THE SINGING HILL

Books by Meindert DeJong

THE

PICTURES BY MAURICE SENDAK

HARPER & ROW, PUBLISHERS,

SINGING HILL

BY MEINDERT DEJONG

NEW YORK AND EVANSTON

TO MAURICE SENDAK,
who illuminates my things,
because we are a pair.

CONTENTS

CHAPTER 1 * THEE—RAYMOND

Ray lived in the country. Of course, his name was really Raymond. Raymond was his baptized name. And he didn't go to school yet.

The minister had baptized him when he was a baby. The minister had sprinkled water over him and had said, "I baptize thee—Raymond."

So Ray was really Raymond, but his big brother, Martin, called him Rim.

Once Ray had asked Martin, "Why do you call me Rim?"

Martin had said, "Oh, I named you after my bicycle wheel. Thee-Rim."

Martin had laughed and laughed.

Imagine when he—Ray—was just a new baby,

1

Martin had already been old enough to sit in church and watch him being baptized. Martin had been there in church when the minister had dripped water from his fingertips and said, "I baptize thee—Raymond."

Martin had been that old! But Martin said, "I was so young then I didn't know about baptism, and it made me mad when the minister dripped water on your little bald head. Man, I was so little then I called you Rim, because I couldn't say Raymond."

Well, that was better than that Martin had named him after a bicycle wheel. Martin had just thought that up about the bicycle wheel. Martin thought that it was funny to say. It wasn't funny.

Still, it was better to be called Rim than to be called Raimie! Shirley did that. Shirley was even older than Martin. "That's sisters for you," Martin always said, "they're mushy." Raimie was a mushy name. It sounded small. It sounded as if you were awfully young and didn't go to school yet.

Of course, he didn't go to school yet, and Mother called him Raimie, too. But somehow it didn't sound mushy when Mother said it.

2

It sounded proper. Just the same he kept telling Mother, "My name is Ray."

Mother would say, "Yes, I know Raimie—Ray. But I like to call you Raimie. It's for short and for young and for nice."

"Dad calls me Ray," he'd told Mother. "When I start to go to school will you start to call me Ray?"

"Oh, I will," Mother had promised. "If that's what you like best."

Of course, he liked Ray the best. Ray was much shorter than Raimie, but it sounded bigger. It was the shortest, but it sounded the biggest. And Dad always called him Ray. Of course, Dad wasn't home much except on Saturdays and Sundays.

Imagine living in the country! They'd all moved into the country only two weeks ago, and now he— Ray—lived in the country. Mother and Shirley and Martin hadn't lived in the country when they were still too young to go to school. Dad had, but that was far away in another state when Dad had been a little boy. It was long ago.

Mother said that the one nice thing about

3

living in the country was that now she would have Raimie with her another whole year. If they had stayed in town, he—Ray—would have been going to school, but here in the country he did not have to go for another year. Mother thought it was wonderful.

Mother didn't like the country. She was afraid of it. She thought that in the country the grass was full of bugs and wriggly, crawly things—and even snakes!

So then Dad had said, oh, well, if Mother felt that way he'd keep the grass cut short around the house, because he, for one, was glad to be living in the country again.

There weren't any snakes in the grass! And imagine living in a great big farmhouse in the country!

Mother said the house was far too big. She said it was an old, rambling, all-over-the-place three-story farmhouse—if you counted the attic. She said it had far too many high, narrow windows that were hard to wash.

But Shirley said it wasn't even a farmhouse —not anymore—and not really, because real farmhouses had barns. All their house had was an old two-stall garage.

4

Martin argued with Shirley that maybe it was a garage now, but it had once been a horse barn. There was even a horse stall left in one end of the garage. So then didn't that make their house a real farmhouse?

Shirley said Martin was arguing like a silly little kid. It didn't matter if there was still a horse stall in the garage. They didn't have a horse, did they? And, anyway, all the horse stable was used for was a storage space for Dad's boxes and samples.

Martin didn't know what to say right away, so Shirley seemed to think she had won the argument.

Ray had to wait four days before he could ask Dad was their house a farmhouse. It was Saturday. He and Dad were in the garage—in the horse stable. Dad sat down on one of the boxes in the stable, so Ray did, too.

"Look at it this way, Ray," Dad had said. "Yes and no. It is a farmhouse, but a farmhouse without a farm and without barns and without farm animals. But all around the house, except for the lawn which I still have to mow, it's a farm. Not our farm—and that's

a good thing, because I'm not a farmer, I'm a salesman. But this farm and all the farms around belong to one man. He bought them all just to raise corn. That's why all you see around our house is one great big cornfield that looks almost like a big, green sea. It's a whole sea of corn!

"But the man who bought all the farms just to raise corn couldn't use all the farmhouses. A man can't live in very many houses at one time, can he? One house was enough for him, so he sold all the others, and I bought this one. So now we have a house in the country. Do you like it in the country, Ray?"

"Oh, I do," he'd told Dad. "I do. . . . And there aren't any snakes in the grass, are there, Dad? The country isn't all full of bugs and wriggly, crawly things?"

Dad had snorted. "That's what your mother imagines, because she doesn't know the country. When you don't know, you imagine all kinds of things. Oh, there are rats and mice, but there are rats and mice in town. There are chipmunks and gophers, but they're quick and nice. There are skunks, but they're slow and mind their own business, and if you mind your

own business and let them alone, they won't bother you. But I'm glad, Ray, you reminded me of those snakes in the grass. Here I'm just sitting, and I've still got to mow the grass and all those snakes in it that your mother imagines. But don't worry, Ray. It'll take a little while and then your mother will know the country, and she'll like it, too."

Dad had jumped up to mow the grass, but Ray had asked him, "Only you and I lived in the country when we were so young we didn't even go to school yet, didn't we, Dad?"

"Right you are," Dad had said loudly, because he was wheeling the rattly mower out of the garage. "Right you are, Ray. I guess that makes you and me the only almost-born farmers in the family."

Then Ray had jumped up and rushed out of the garage just to run up and down and back and forth with Dad and the mower, because it was Saturday, and Dad was home, and home was in the country. There were no snakes in the grass, and everything was wonderful.

8

CHAPTER 2 * SCALP AND SKELETON

Martin and Shirley had to go to the new school in the country right away. They'd all moved to the country on Saturday, and the next Monday Shirley and Martin had to start school. The first week Martin and Shirley didn't walk—Mother took them in the car, and Ray went along. After the first day there wasn't much new to see from the road they lived on, or from the crossroad that led to the school road, or from the school road itself. It was all corn.

Of course, there were a few houses and barns

9

in among the corn. At the corner of the cross-road and the school road there was a field with sheep, and behind it a field with cows, but except for that everything was one huge corn-field. Martin said that their road and the school road were exactly a mile apart. "So that corn-field is a whole mile of corn wide," Martin said. "And I don't know how long it is, but all you see is corn. Around our house, around the school—it's all corn. Pretty soon it'll be sticking out of our ears."

That made Shirley giggle. "Ears of corn sticking out of our ears—ears out of ears," she said. Then she giggled some more.

Mother didn't think it was funny. "Now must you giggle about it all the way to school?" she said. "It wasn't *that* funny."

"Why does it always have to be Martin who makes the funny jokes?" Shirley said. She pressed her lips shut as if she weren't going to say another word all the way to school. Nobody paid any attention.

Martin talked to Mother about the creek that ran along the road to school. He pointed to where the creek almost disappeared among the trees and bushes behind a little white house. The house was all in the trees. It was awfully old, but so were the two old people that lived in it, Martin said. Martin guessed the old woman couldn't walk, because she always sat in a rocking chair at the window.

Behind the house under the trees there was an old shed that had fallen flat over the creek. Mother looked at it. "There's nothing so flat as that fallen shed," Mother said. "It looks as if it just sighed and laid itself down to rest."

Martin said that now the shed made a good bridge for the old people to get over the creek. Then he said, oh, wouldn't it be fun to sail boats under the shed? There they'd go like a train into a tunnel. They'd shoot from under the shed and race down the creek all the way to school, because the creek ran behind the school, too.

Shirley forgot that she hadn't been going to say anything. She said in a surly voice that it sure wasn't much of a school, even if it had a creek running behind it, because it had just two rooms. And Martin was younger than she, but Martin had to be right in the same room with her.

"I don't like it," Shirley said.

13

Martin whispered in Ray's ear that he didn't like it either. Martin said girls were tattletales, and you couldn't do anything with Shirley in the same room. It was no fun.

The third day on the way back with Mother from taking Shirley and Martin to school, the old man that lived in the little white house was outside in the yard standing by the fallen-down shed. Suddenly, for no reason, Ray waved and shouted, "Hi, Grandpa!"

The old man looked up, surprised, but in the house the old woman in the rocking chair waved back. Mother looked surprised, too. Then she said, "That was a nice thing to do, Raimie. Always be nice to old people."

She didn't say why, but after that Ray waved and yelled "Hi" every day.

The last day of that first week the old man was outside again. Ray yelled, "Hi, Grandpa!" The old man did not look up. He was standing by the creek again, looking down at the fallen shed. The old lady in the rocker saw Ray wave, so she laughed and smiled and waved back at him. But the fallen shed—well, that was sad.

After that day Mother did not take Shirley

14

and Martin to school anymore. Martin and Shirley wanted to walk. The kids in the new school had shown them a short cut. It went through the cornfield and along the creek. Martin said it was fun going to school now. Fun going to school and fun coming back— double fun, because on the way to school and on the way back he and Shirley played in the corn.

But Shirley said the corn was so tall and

high above you, you couldn't see anything but the sky and the corn. And the rows went on and on and were so endless, why, you could easily get lost in the corn. You'd starve to death, and there you'd be—a skeleton!

"You could eat the corn instead of starving to a skeleton," Martin said. "What do you want to scare Rim for?"

"Oh, you!" Shirley said. She flounced away. Then Martin told Ray the corn wasn't scary at all. Shirley just scared herself. "She makes up scary things, and then believes them herself!" Martin was disgusted with Shirley. "Why, it's fun running down those long rows of corn!"

Martin told Ray that he and Shirley played Indian in the corn. He'd let Shirley get way ahead, sneak after her and track her down, and then he'd scalp her with his wooden tomahawk.

"What's scalp?" Ray said.

"Gee, Rim," Martin said, "don't you know anything? Scalp means cut your hair off and take most of the top of your head along with it. Of course, I don't really cut Shirley's hair off—it's just make-believe with a wooden tomahawk I made. But it's so real to Shirley, she screams and screams and almost dies."

16

They didn't know Shirley had stayed in the garage around the corner of the horse stable. Now she came back. "I don't either, Martin Garroway!" she said, and she stamped her foot. "The stuff you tell your little brother! And you don't play fair. I never get a turn to scalp you. You always have to be the Indian with the tomahawk."

Martin said it was, too, fair. "Listen, Rim, can I help it I haven't got long hair? You've got to have long hair to grab when you scalp somebody, and I've got a crew cut."

It was Saturday, but Dad hadn't come home. Shirley and Martin had nothing to do. It was raining, so they were talking in the garage. They were talking to Ray. At least they made believe they were talking to him, but sometimes Ray thought his big brother and sister just quarreled with each other while making believe they were talking to him.

Secretly Ray sided with Shirley about the Indian game. It made the top of his head tingle to think of being scalped in the big cornfield. He was glad that the last time in the barber shop, just before they had moved, Dad had got him a crew cut. Mother hadn't liked it. He really hadn't either, but now he was glad for next year. Next year when he started school Martin couldn't sneak up and grab him by the hair and scalp him—he had a crew cut just like Martin's. Next year they'd both scalp Shirley!

Mother didn't know they were in the garage sitting in the horse stable. Mother was busy in the house. It was raining hard.

Shirley said that hound-and-hare was a much better game than the Indian game. She explained to Ray that in the hound-and-hare game, if you were the hound you had to catch the hare, but you didn't have to scalp anything and make things all scary. Besides, in this game she could take turns with Martin to be the hound or the hare. She didn't always have to be the scalped Indian.

Ray looked at Shirley's hair while she was talking, and his mouth must have been open, because Martin suddenly said, "Rim, close your mouth. A hare is a rabbit. It's got nothing to do with the hair on your head."

"Oh," Ray said, and was glad for Shirley, because he wouldn't like to be scalped all the time either. Hound-and-hare sounded like a good game. Shirley said it didn't have to be played only in the corn like the Indian game.

Hound-and-hare went all over the hills and fields, through the corn, back of Grandpa's house, and along the creek all the way to school. It went wherever the hare went.

Martin said, "Yeah, it's a real good game."

But Shirley said that when you were playing hound-and-hare it was more like history. You really were like a pioneer. You blazed trails the way the pioneers way back in early America had to do to find their way through the endless woods back to their early settlements.

Shirley said it was all in her history book. Shirley had history in school, but not Martin, so Martin just had to let Shirley talk.

"What's blazing?" Ray asked Shirley.

Then Shirley sat up and made herself tall and straight on the box so as to look like a teacher. "In a way, Raimie," she said, "blazing is something like scalping, except you do it to the bark on trees—not to the top of somebody's head. Blazing means chopping a slice of bark off the side of a tree. Then when the pioneer turned around to go back to his early settlement through the dark, shadowy forest, he just followed the marks on the trees he'd made himself on the way out."

Martin interrupted Shirley. "See, Rim, the

19

settlers used hatchets, but Indians used toma-
hawks, but it's about the same difference."

Martin wanted to show he knew something,
too, but it was really Shirley that knew, because
she was older, and she was going to be a teacher
when she grew up. Teachers had to know
everything, Shirley said.

In among all the hard sounds of rain on the
garage roof, they suddenly realized Mother was
calling them. "Shirl—eeee, Mar—tin!"

Shirley and Martin ran to the open garage
door, but Ray hadn't been called, so he just
walked to the door.

"We're here," Shirley yelled back to Mother.
"In the garage."

"Oh," Mother said. "Raimie, too? I got to
worrying you might be playing in the corn in
all this rain. . . . Oh, there you are, Raimie.
Don't ever go wandering in the cornfield alone,
will you?"

"No, Mother," Ray said from behind Martin
and Shirley. He really meant it. He didn't want
to be found a skeleton.

Ray and Martin were lucky. Mother wanted
only Shirley. She hadn't made her bed.

"Hunh," Martin said, "and here girls are

supposed to be so neat. I made my bed!"

"I wouldn't want to be found a skeleton," Ray told Martin, looking out at the rain over the cornfield.

Martin hee-hawed. "That crazy Shirley," he said. "Is she wild. Why, you couldn't get lost! There are all kinds of lanes that crisscross through that cornfield. You see, Rim, they need them for the tractors and trucks, else how could they get in that field? Well, then, even if you were in the middle of the highest corn, all you'd do is walk down one of the corn rows till you came to a lane. You'd walk down the lane till you came to a road, then you'd go home down the road."

Martin made it sound as simple as pie.

"Look," Martin said. "See that broken-down apple tree on the side of the road just beyond our yard? Just on the other side of that apple tree there's a lane that goes into the cornfield, and it's the best one of all, because it's even got fences. And right at the foot of one of the fence posts there's a skunk hole. Shirley and I stuck it full of cornstalks. And every morning we go to school we rattle the cornstalks and yell like crazy down the hole to make the skunk

21

mad. Skunks are slow and can't catch you. But man, you ought to see Shirley. After she yells into the skunk hole, she goes on screaming all the way up the lane. She shakes all over!"

"If the skunk caught her, would he bite her?" Ray wanted to know.

"Gee whiz, Rim, no!" Martin said, disgusted. "No! Skunks spray an awful scent and swish it all over you with their tails. You choke to death, almost. You can't go near people for weeks, and they have to bury your clothes forever, and you have to take baths in vinegar, because otherwise even your mother can't stand you."

Ray couldn't believe it. Sometimes when Shirley wasn't around to say it wasn't so, Martin talked awfully big. You couldn't take a bath in vinegar—your skin would come off!

Shirley suddenly was at the back door yelling, "Martin, you've got to come in the house right away!"

"Why?" Martin yelled back. "I made my bed."

"Yeah, but you didn't put your clothes away, and I've got my room all picked up! Raimie, you've got to come, too. Mother says so."

Oh, Martin was mad at Shirley. He was so

mad he wouldn't come right away. "You can just bet she tattled on me," he said to Ray. "You don't tattle, do you?"

"Oh, no!" Ray said quickly. He wanted to ask Martin if Martin would show him the skunk hole, because when Martin was mad at Shirley he sometimes would do all kinds of things for him he otherwise wouldn't do.

Then Martin said, "Look, Rim, I want to show you something." They ran back to the horse stable, and Martin showed Ray two empty sardine cans and an oval kippered-herring can that he'd hidden between Dad's boxes. "You know what those are?" Martin said. "Those are Shirley's and my boats that we're going to sail down the creek. The sardine cans are the Nina and Pinta, and the kippered-herring one is the Santa Maria. Those were Columbus's ships when he discovered America. The Santa Maria was the flagship. That's why the big kippered-herring can has to be the Santa Maria. Monday on our way to school we're going to sail them down the creek, then after school we're going to go all the way down the creek to see how far they went before they sank. I thought of it, and I found the tin cans, but

do you know that crazy Shirley? She wouldn't play with them unless we washed them first. Didn't want to sail boats that smelled oily and fishy. Girls! But listen, Rim, don't you tell Shirley—and Mother, either! It's only a little creek. You can even step over it, but you know Mother. She'd think we'd drown in a creek you can step over!"

Ray forgot to promise Martin out loud. He was busy running the names of the sardine cans through his mind to remember them. Nina and Pinta—Nina and Pinta. When you said them inside yourself, they were words that were almost as sweet on your tongue as a grape. They weren't sharp, mean words like "scalp" and "skeleton."

Mother came to the back door and called them. She sounded angry. Ray and Martin both ran, but Martin said out of the side of his mouth, "Don't you tell now, or I'll—I'll scalp you!"

While Mother was scolding Martin for not coming immediately, Ray suddenly had a wonderful thought. Monday morning when Martin and Shirley went to school he would secretly follow them to watch just exactly what they did in the lane at the skunk hole with all those cornstalks stuck in it. Mother, still angry with Martin, saw Ray smiling to himself. "And what are you standing there grinning about like a cat full of canaries? Hop to it! Get cleaned up and dressed. We're all going to town for new clothes. I haven't been able to get around to it with this moving, but I guess it's the best thing to do in the rain, and your father's not coming home till tomorrow. It's better anyway than you three sitting quarreling in the garage!"

25

Mother gave Ray a spank on the seat of his pants to send him up the stairs.

"Ha-ha," he said, "didn't even hurt any!" He all but danced up the stairs, because Monday he'd follow Shirley and Martin to the skunk hole in the lane.

CHAPTER 3 * NEW HAT

Oh, it was Sunday! Sure, it was Sunday. Shirley and Martin wouldn't be going to school, and he—Ray—couldn't follow them down the lane to the skunk hole. There, as he awoke, was the thought and the disappointment.

Dad must have come home during the night. Ray hadn't heard him come, but now he heard his big voice downstairs. It was Sunday morning, the day for going to church with Dad, and the day for the new hat.

Mother had bought the new straw hat almost the last thing in the big department store Saturday afternoon. They were walking out of the store when Mother suddenly picked the hat off a table and fitted it on his head. "Your dad,"

27

she'd said, "is going to have new shoes, so you should have a new Sunday hat for going to church with him."

When Ray got down to the kitchen it was so late he had to eat alone—everybody'd already had breakfast. Mother and Shirley and Martin were extra early because they were excited about their new clothes. Early as it was, they were already getting dressed for church, even though they never went to the first service— just he and Dad went to the early service.

Dad was making a big, make-believe fuss about all the new clothes, while all he'd got was new shoes. "I suppose," he said to Ray, "you got left out altogether."

Ray couldn't answer with a mouth full of cereal, so he jumped up and ran off to show Dad the new hat. He put it on before he walked back into the kitchen. He held his neck stiff and the top of his head flat so as not to jiggle and drop the hat just as he was showing it to Dad. He was proud of his new hat. The hat had a speckled band, and a small, very bright yellow feather poking up out of the speckled band.

Dad didn't say much about the new hat. He was teasing Shirley. "Look at her," he said to

28

Ray. "Look at all of them getting decked out in all those new clothes, and what do you and I get between the two of us? Two shoes and one hat. All they took care of was your head and my feet. I guess you're just going to have to ride on my shoulders when you and I walk into church this morning. That way, with your new hat and my new shoes, people maybe won't notice the raggedy clothes we have to wear between them."

Dad didn't really care, of course, that all he had was new shoes, so he—Ray—didn't care that all he had was the new hat. But Shirley couldn't get her new dress twisted just right, and she was already so annoyed with Dad's teasing that she sputtered and sputtered.

"Oh, Shirley, haven't you learned yet?" Mother said, sweeping by in her new dress. "It's all done to get your goat. Pay it no attention. . . . It seems to me, Martin, that with a new suit you ought to tie your tie better."

"You know, Ray," Dad said very loudly, "with all this dressing fuss, you and I had better get from underfoot and go to the early service this morning."

"As if you two didn't always go to the early service," Shirley yelped. And then she said all kinds of things to herself under her breath.

Later, when Ray and Dad were ready for church and they went to the garage to get the car, Dad suddenly thought that he had to check something among his boxes and samples stacked in the horse stable. He pulled some boxes out of the way, and there came the two sardine cans tumbling down. Dad reached between the boxes and pulled out the kippered-herring can. "Who put these here?" he asked.

"I didn't," Ray said.

"Well, then they're Shirley's or Martin's," Dad said. "I'll bet you they use them for boats to sail in the creek that runs along their school road."

Ray nodded, amazed that Dad had guessed. But he hadn't told! He hadn't run to Dad and tattled. Dad had found the cans! Dad had guessed! Still, Martin would never believe he hadn't told. And Martin had said he'd scalp him if he tattled. Ray thought of telling Dad about Martin's threatening to scalp him. But that *would* be tattling!

For a moment it was a problem. But Dad wasn't angry at all about the tin cans. He even grinned about it, and that made everything much better. "Imagine, Shirley and Martin liking to sail tin cans! As a kid there was nothing I liked better. Flat tin cans like these were the best. You can sink them. . . . Hey!" Dad said. "We're way early. Let's you and I go sail these cans down that creek for a little while. It'd be fun again."

It was a good thing Shirley had first washed the cans, because Dad just shoved the kippered-herring can down in one pocket of his Sunday pants and shoved the two sardine cans in the other pocket.

"Those are the Nina and the Pinta," Ray told Dad.

"What'd you say?" Dad asked, surprised. "Oh, that's right—Columbus's ships! Let's see now. What was the name of the other one again? The flagship?"

Ray tried, but he just couldn't think of it. Dad frowned and wrinkled his face, but he couldn't think of it. It made Dad impatient with himself, but that didn't help either. Then Dad shook his head and said, "Ah, what's the

31

difference, we'll sail them anyway. Let's go, Columbus."

But it did make a difference, for all the way in the car he and Dad just sat trying to think of the name of the kippered-herring-can flagship. Dad even muttered aloud to himself, "The Nina, the Pinta. Now what was the name of the other one? Nuts!"

Dad stopped the car at the corner of the crossroad and the school road. The sheep weren't in the corner field this day, but a herd of cows was in the field behind it. The creek ran through the corner field near the back fence. Ray was surprised. He hadn't seen that in the week when he and Mother had taken Martin and Shirley to school in the car, but Dad knew.

There was a wire fence around the field—square blocks of wire you could just shove your toes into and climb like a ladder. But with all the tin cans in the pockets, Dad's trousers were too tight for climbing. He first had to throw the tin cans over the fence. Ray climbed the fence slowly, because he had to hold his neck stiff and his head flat so as not to jiggle the new hat off his head. "Watch it," Dad said. "Don't

32

be so careful for the hat that you rip your pants. That'd be hard to explain to your mother—a rip in the pants from going to church!"

Ray had just thrown one leg over the fence, but he had to sit a moment astride it, he was laughing so hard. Dad stood laughing with the three tin cans in his hands. A car came down the road so slowly and quietly it surprised both of them. Dad dropped his tin cans, then waved very innocently at the car. "That was the preacher!" he said in a hoarse whisper. "I didn't know he lived out this way. Me standing here with my tin-can fleet, and you riding a fence on Sunday morning. What must he think?"

They waited until the car was out of sight, then Dad laughed and said, "Well, we're here now. Let's go sail our boats anyway. Here, you launch the fleet while I hunt up some stones for ammunition. Then we'll follow our boats, and try to bombard and sink them. Otherwise we're likely to follow them so long, we won't get to church at all."

It was so early the grass was still wet with dew. "Your new shoes!" Ray warned Dad.

Dad looked down at his shiny new shoes.

"Oh, I guess it won't hurt. It's short, sheep-nibbled grass," he said, and wandered away looking for stones.

Even though it was a narrow, little creek, the clay bank went down so straight and steep Ray had to stoop far down to put the two sardine cans in the water. Behind him Dad called out, "Hey, Columbus, the kippered-herring can first—that's the flagship, you know. Then the Nina and the Pinta."

He felt stupid to have put the Nina and Pinta sardine cans in the creek ahead of the Santa Maria. But there was the name of the flagship! It had come—just like that! Ray jerked around and yelled to Dad, "The Santa Maria! The kippered-herring can is the Santa Maria!" Turning around so fast joggled the new hat loose. It fell bottom up in the creek, and shot away on the current. It was so light it raced past the Santa Maria and Nina and Pinta. The little yellow feather dragged through the water like a rudder. For a moment Ray sat stunned, but then he jumped up. He yelled, "Dad, Dad —my hat!" He tore along the creek after his hat.

Dad raced across the pasture, came pounding along the creek behind Ray, passed him, but it

34

was too late. The hat swirled under the fence
into the cow pasture. Right behind the hat the
Nina and Pinta and Santa Maria shot under
the fence.

"Stay here," Dad said. He started to climb
the woven-wire fence.

"Dad, there are cows in there," Ray warned.
There was quite a herd of cows grazing at the
far end of the field behind the fence. Dad, with
one leg thrown over the jiggling wire fence,

looked at the faraway cows. The cows didn't even look up from their grazing.

"Cows are peaceable animals," Dad said, and jumped down into the field.

Not far beyond the fence the creek disappeared into a clump of thick bushes and trees. The new hat disappeared among the bushes; right behind it the three tin cans went out of sight. Ray reached his hands way up as if to climb the fence. Dad saw it. "No, Ray," he said quietly. Then he ran toward the bushes after the hat.

Ray stood with his hands stretched up watching through the fence. Strangely, there was a rumble as of thunder. No, it was more like a truck going over a bridge. But the sound wasn't like that either. It ran and rumbled along the ground as if it came out of the ground. Then the bushes parted. A big bull pushed out of the bushes! He stood facing Dad, stood pawing and rumbling. He threw dirt all over his own back with his pawing front hoof. He rumbled horribly out of his throat, and his head went lower and lower until his horns touched the ground.

Dad stood there like stone, stiff and straight,

36

facing the bull. The bull must have seen Ray
and Dad playing at the creek in the sheep
pasture. He'd left his cows, and he'd skulked
in the bushes like a mean dog, waiting. There
they stood—Dad and the bull.

Suddenly Dad turned, and ran like mad back
to the fence. The bull roared after him, head
and horns down. He thundered over the field.
The pounding of his hoofs was a hollow, terrible sound in the grass.

Dad threw himself out ahead of the bull in

big, scared lunges. His face was still, his eyes were big and white and scared. He threw one look back over his shoulder. The bull was right behind him. Dad began to zigzag and twist; he began to jump back and forth over the creek—monstrous long jumps back and forth over the narrow creek. But then the bull did, too! The bull plunged back and forth over the creek. He couldn't twist his big, thick body around that fast. He stumbled. He stumbled and coughed and went down to one knee, but he heaved himself up—came up and over the creek in one great, terrible lunge. Then for some reason he stopped. He roared, and his eyes rolled red and bloodshot in his head, but he stood confused.

Dad threw one look over his shoulder, saw the bull stop, and came racing to the fence where Ray clung. But now that Dad ran straight, the bull came on straight. Dad would never get over the fence in time. Never, never, never. It was as if Ray had turned to stone, as if he couldn't make a sound, and still he felt himself jumping up and down against the fence. He heard himself screaming. "Never, Dad! Never, never, never!" He pulled himself up the fence by his upstretched hands, and he screamed, "Never, never!"

The bull heard him; the bull saw him jumping up and down. Suddenly he turned his wild, red eyes away from Dad, and turned them on Ray. He came roaring, plunging, thundering. He hit the fence and it rattled and shook. Ray was knocked away from the rocking fence, but Dad scrambled up and over. Ray fell and lay on his back, looking up at the bull ramming the fence again and again with his horrible ugly head with the horns and red eyes.

Then Dad picked him up and flung him over his shoulder, and ran across the pasture back to the roadside fence and the car. Thrown over Dad's shoulder that way, Ray could still see the bull. The bull had caught his big crooked horns in the fence. The bull was fighting the fence, jerking and ramming his big head to get his horns free. The whole fence rattled all around the pasture, and back there the fence posts wobbled and rocked back and forth.

Dad never stopped running. He even climbed the roadside fence with Ray flung over his shoulder. He never stopped until he got to the car. He wrenched the car door open, just stooped, and let Ray clamber off his shoulder. Then Dad just let himself fall into the seat, and sat there breathing hard. At last, he swallowed and caught his breath. "There, now I feel safe," he said in between breaths. "Two fences between us and that beast, and we're in the car." He sat for a long time looking at the bull rocking the fence and the fence posts. Suddenly Dad leaned out of the car. "Yeah, you!" he yelled across the field. "I hope you stay caught in that fence, and it rains on you and your ugly head for two weeks."

That made Ray want to laugh, because it felt so safe to be in the car with Dad, and Dad yelling crazy things like that at the distant bull. But instead of laughing, he began crying. He was crying!

Dad let him cry for a while. Then he said, "Hey, guess we'll have to tell your mother they had to use your new hat in church to take the collection, and there was so much money the bottom fell out!"

It was such a funny thing to say right then Ray wanted to laugh, but he couldn't stop crying. He opened his hands to show Dad the red welts from clutching the wire fence. He

acted as if he were crying about that, but Dad
knew he wasn't, for Dad said quietly, "Look,
you and I had better get to church. It'll seem
good to sit somewhere where it's nice and safe
and quiet."

Ray swallowed his last sob, and nodded his
head.

CHAPTER 4 * THE FOUR SECRETS

It was safe and peaceful in church. The minister's slow voice went on and on, sure and long and calm. Ray sat close to Dad. Dad had his arm flung along the back of the pew behind Ray. Every now and then his fingers found Ray's shoulder to give it a little reassuring pinch.

It was queer. You sat safe and still, but inside of you the quaking went on. The minister's slow words came down to you as if on a long slant from the high platform. You heard the words but they were meaningless, because inside of you you still heard the words that Dad had yelled at the bull. "I hope you stay caught in that fence, and it rains on you and your

42

ugly head for two whole weeks." And even here in church you were still scared of the bull.

Ray looked up at Dad as if to ask him a question. His father noticed, and shook his head ever so slightly. His fingers nipped Ray's shoulder. But the nip didn't help, because it would be awful even for an awful bull to stay caught in a fence for two weeks. He wouldn't be able to eat for two weeks! He'd be weak and hungry. Oh, he'd be hungry! And the rain raining down on him.

Dad must have noticed Ray's worried face, because he stooped down and whispered, "Don't worry, we'll get your hat back."

Ray sat up straight. Get the hat back? That was a strange thing for Dad to say. It was a strange and a worrisome thing if it meant that Dad intended to go back to the creek and the field with the bull. Ray pondered it, and his mind was so busy with it that suddenly, surprisingly the church was stirring and people were getting up to sing. After the singing the church let out.

Outside in the church parking lot Dad talked loud and long with three men. They laughed a great deal, and three times Dad started away, but each time he turned back to say something more. He was telling the men about the bull. It looked as if Dad were never going to leave. "Dad," Ray said anxiously, "what will we tell Mom about my hat?"

His face got red, because all the men looked down at him. But Dad said, "Oh, we're going back to get your hat."

One of the men touched Ray on his bare head, and grinned and said, "That is, if that bull isn't wearing it between those horns of his."

All the men laughed, but Ray laughed only as long as they kept looking at him. He was worried. Maybe Dad had just said that about going back to get the hat to say something because he—Ray—had talked right into the talk of the men. But he'd whispered it in church, too. And now it must be Dad was really leaving, because he took Ray by the hand, then said it again: "Come on, Ray, let's go get your hat."

Ray hung back. "Are we really going back to the bull?"

"Why, no, of course not! At least we won't be going into that field with the bull. We'll stay far away from that field. We've got to start

44

beyond that field and follow the creek if we're going to find your hat. But in no time we'll be miles from that bull."

"Dad," Ray asked worriedly, "could we first ride along that field to see if the bull is still caught in the fence?"

"Oh, sure," Dad said. "I want to know that, too. If he's still caught, I'll want to notify the farmer that owns him."

Oh, it was wonderful what Dad had said. Now it wasn't scary at all to go back.

When they got to the corner field, the bull wasn't caught in the fence anymore. The fence wasn't lying flat. The fence stood straight. The bull was way back in the field where the cows had been in the morning. He was grazing peacefully with his cows. From the road Dad blew his horn at the distant bull. Then Ray cupped his hands to his mouth and yelled, "Hey you— you ugly beast, you!"

"I just called him that for fun," he told Dad. "I'm glad he got his horns out of the fence. He was mean but I didn't want him to go hungry while the rain rained on him for two whole weeks."

"Oh?" Dad said, surprised. "Is that what was

45

bothering you in church? Well, I don't want that either, Ray. Goodness, I just yelled because it felt good to be yelling; the same way you yelled at the bull just now."

Ray was glad Dad had explained it. But then Dad said, "You know, Ray, right here I ought to tell you. It was a mighty good thing you distracted the bull this morning with your yelling and jumping. Otherwise, I'm afraid he would have caught me before I could have made it over the fence. And his horns looked awfully hard. And so did his head."

"Oh, awful," Ray said like a big man in a big man's calm way, but inside he felt so proud he was almost bursting. But then it also felt good to snuggle up to Dad, and tell him honestly, "Dad, I didn't know I was yelling and jumping. I didn't even know I'd let go of the fence when he came at me. I thought I couldn't let go. It was so awful, his big head and his red eyes rolling in his head. Then he hit the fence, but I had let go!" He had to stop, because just talking about it made him start to shake again. He hurried to think up something else to say. "Dad," he said, "if we do find the hat, I'll hold it out of the car window on the way home so it will dry."

"Well, Ray," Dad said as he started the car, "let's not count our chickens, cross our bridges, dry our hats. Well, anyway, let's first find the hat."

Oh, that was funny. And, oh, it was cozy in the car with Dad, and the road and the fields all sunny. The car turned the corner and went down the school road, and then there was the creek again. Where the creek almost touched the high road before it turned away back into the fields again, Dad stopped the car and they got out. Dad immediately went sliding and half running down the steep road bank to the creek, but Ray waited on the side of the high road.

Everything was so big and so still in the Sunday silence that now he was out of the car Ray didn't really want to follow the creek—not even to get the hat back. Somehow the creek rushing below the road bank seemed to be making the same hollow, down-in-the-ground sounds the bull had made with his pounding hoofs. Ray looked back along the road. It must be a long way from the bull.

Dad stepped over the creek. He looked up

47

and saw that Ray was still standing at the side of the road. "Come on," Dad said, "if we're going to find your hat."

Ray had to hurry and slip and slide down the steep bank. Dad didn't wait. He set such a pace along the winding creek it was hard to keep up with him. Ray dogtrotted on behind his father trying hard to think of something to make his dad stop and wait for him. The fields were so still, and behind him the creek made sounds that made you think all the time that something was coming running. He had to think of something to make his dad wait. "How far does this creek go?" Ray thought to ask at last. "How far does this creek go anyway, Dad?"

Dad didn't stop. "To the sea," he yelled over his shoulder.

The sea? What sea? Ray stopped to ponder it, and forgot to run. "What sea, Dad?"

That stopped Dad. He turned around and spread his hands wide. Ray seized the chance to trot up to him. "Should I know?" Dad said. "Somewhere there's a sea, and some way, somehow, this creek eventually winds up in that sea. This creek will go into some bigger creek, and that will go into some river, and that river into some bigger river, and always into a bigger and bigger river, and the biggest river at last winds up in the sea. See it? There goes your hat with the yellow feather across the sea. There's nothing for it. We're going to have to fish your hat out of this creek. We just haven't the time before Mother and Martin and Shirley get home to fish it out of the sea."

Oh, that was a good joke in the big, wide, quiet country. It was good to be standing with Dad, laughing with him on the bank of the creek Dad had made the joke about. It was funny, it was strange, but it was wonderful, too, to be standing on the bank of a little creek that somehow, some way, went to the sea. It was a joke, it was wondrously funny, but it was wondrously serious at the same time. Now it was good to be here.

Dad was looking up and down the creek, and suddenly he sprinted away. He got down on one knee, stooped, and came up with the two dripping sardine cans. Ray saw something glint in the water a little farther down the creek. He dashed around Dad, and there it was on the bottom of the creek—the kippered-herring can, the Santa Maria. He held it up.

49

"Good boy," Dad said. "Now we know that if our Columbus fleet got this far, the hat must have gone farther down the creek, because the hat can't sink. The tin cans didn't get snagged, so your hat didn't get snagged somewhere against the creek bank either. Come on, before it gets to that sea."

They ran along the creek. They came around the bottom of a hill. Around the hill the creek dipped away into a shadowy clump of tall trees and thick bushes. Ray ran after Dad and grabbed his hand. Dad hurried along, but Ray dragged and hung back. Dad noticed. "Tired? Side ache? Oh, Ray! There isn't a bull in every clump of trees and behind every bush."

But now Dad walked more slowly himself. They both looked hard at the bushes under the shadowy trees. The creek was dark under the trees. Ray listened for sounds to come out of the bushes. Dad seemed to be listening, too.

Then there actually was a sound under the trees! But Dad went right on. He dragged Ray along. They went around a clump of bushes. There was an old man under the trees. He was coughing. That was the sound they had heard!

The old man was stooped over, and couldn't

50

seem to stop coughing. It was a desperate sound under the trees. The old man straightened up, and stood gasping and fanning himself with a hat. "Dad!" Ray whispered. It was the new hat—his hat. Now that the old man had straightened up, Ray saw it was Grandpa. "Dad, it's Grandpa!" Why, this was the clump of trees behind Grandpa's house. There was the little white house, and beyond the trees there lay the shed fallen down over the creek. Some-

how it was all different—it was even strange—
to be in among the trees that you'd seen only
from a car on the high road.

Grandpa wiped his eyes and his mouth.
"Why, it's the little boy who always yells 'Hi,
Grandpa!' from the car," he said. "Then I
imagine this must be your hat that came down
the creek about an hour ago. I caught it just
before it went under the shed. Must be yours,
sonny, hunh?"

Grandpa looked at Dad with the tin cans in
his hands. He smiled a little. "Been playing
in the creek, boys?" he said to Dad.

Dad grinned and shoved the tin cans in his
pockets. Grandpa handed Ray the hat. "Had it
hanging from a tree limb to dry," he explained.
"But I got a coughing spell, and used it for a
fan."

"Say 'Thank you,' Ray," Dad said.

"Thank you, Grandpa," Ray said.

Dad walked over to the fallen shed. "Caved
in, I see," he said to the old man. "I'm Ray's
dad."

"Just like that, of a night," the old man said.
"There it lay in the morning."

"Couldn't it be put back up?" Dad said. "Or
don't you need it?"

"Yes and no," Grandpa said. "I sold my little farm to the man that raises all these miles of corn. I just kept the house and yard, and the shed for the old horse. But I don't need the horse anymore. And the shed just lay down one night."

Grandpa pointed to the hill around which Ray and Dad had come. "Over there I keep the old horse." Ray and Dad looked, but there wasn't much to be seen from under the trees, except the bottom of the hill and the tall corn going up it. "The man that bought my farm and all the other farms for corn let me keep a little hilltop pasture for my horse," Grandpa explained. "The top of the hill was too steep and sandy anyway for raising corn. Let's say I got the hilltop up and beyond where his plows and tractors and big machinery would go. Well, I put a fence around it, and a little grass grows. Even so, it was kind. He didn't have to do it. But I guess he saw it was even harder for me to part with my old horse than it was to part with my farm."

"I understand," Dad said. "But come winter you'll need the shed, won't you, if you want to keep the horse?"

It was serious talk between men. Ray kept

53

straightening the yellow feather that was still in the hatband. It had curled from being in the water.

"I guess I shouldn't have kept the horse," Grandpa said. "I mean, even if I did raise the shed—winter is coming—Grandma can't walk, and I'm full of rheumatism, and there's my asthma—it'll be a chore just to go through the snow to the shed. . . ." Talking about coughing, Grandpa began to cough again. Then he stood, spent. He leaned against a tree.

Dad patted Grandpa's arm. "It seems to me something could be done about that shed." Dad walked over and pulled at a corner of the fallen shed, as if he could lift it and set it up straight right away. "It shouldn't be too much work to set it up, and then brace it up. Maybe some Saturday, as soon as we're a little better settled. We've only just moved here."

Grandpa watched him. "It's fine of you to think so. But you're busy in your own life. Things talk themselves done very easily, but everything takes time, and time is hard to find in everybody's busy life."

Grandpa turned away from the shed and Dad, and looked at Ray. "We don't see you go

54

by in the car anymore," he said. "Grandma often talks about it. She just has to sit and sit. There isn't too much to see on the road, and you always waved."

"Oh, I don't go to school yet," Ray explained. "But next year I'll be coming by every day."

Dad looked at his watch. "I'd like to have a look at the school, now that we're this far," he said. "I haven't seen it yet. Look," he said to Grandpa, "Ray and I go to church together every Sunday. So how about it if on the way back we stop in for a little visit with you and Grandma. We can do that, and I'll see what I can do about the shed."

"Yes, do that," Grandpa said. "It'd be so good for Grandma." He turned and walked to the house as if he were going to tell Grandma right away.

"Ah," Dad said, as he and Ray walked on along the creek, "your mother mentioned to me how sad it seemed—that fallen shed and the two old lonely people. Remember with me, Ray, that we do that of a Sunday—stop by."

"And, Dad, are you really going to put up the shed for Grandpa?"

"I'd sure like to," Dad said. "I'd like to do something for them. I guess you get pretty helpless when you get old and half sick." He looked at his watch again. "Hey, we'd better have a quick look at that school, and then hurry back. Otherwise Mother and Martin and Shirley will be home before us."

When they got to the school, Dad held Ray up and stood him right on the window sill so they both could look inside the schoolroom. There wasn't too much to see. The room was full of desks and seats, and there were blackboards all around. In one corner there was an old, oval table with washpans on it and pails under it. In the other corner there was a sort of furnace stove.

"It sure isn't much," Dad said. "But I hear they've got a good teacher, and that's what counts. And you'll do all right any place, already knowing such things as Nina and Pinta and Santa Maria."

In the schoolroom a mouse suddenly scampered from under one of the seats, and scurried out of sight among the pails under the oval table. Seeing the mouse made Ray think of the skunk hole in the lane. "Dad, are skunks mean?"

"Now where did that suddenly come from—what goes on in that mind of yours?" Dad said, and took Ray down from the window sill. "No, skunks aren't mean, but they are to be treated with respect. A skunk wants to be let alone, so if you ever see one—let him alone. Just keep your distance and go your way, and he'll keep his distance and go his way. Why do you ask? Did you see one?"

"No," Ray said, "but Shirley and Martin found a skunk hole in the lane, and they stuck it full of cornstalks so the skunk can't come out, and they yell down the hole every day to make the skunk mad."

"Those crazy kids," Dad said, "do they do that? What do they think? That a skunk just sits there at the bottom of a hole because they stuck some cornstalks in it? There'll be other openings to that skunk's den, if it is a skunk den, and if there is a skunk there. But if it's the hole at one of the fence posts in the lane that I think you mean, then it's just an empty, abandoned woodchuck hole. Crazy kids! Yelling their heads off down an empty hole."

Suddenly Dad looked at his watch. "Hey, now it's really late. Race you to the car! We'd

57

better go back by way of the road, and we'd better run if we're going to get home before Mother and Martin and Shirley. You realize, Ray, that we've got to keep it a secret about the bull, and about your hat, too—for your mother's sake. It would scare her half to death if she knew a bull had chased me, and then she'd worry even more about living in the country among snakes and bulls. Come on, let's get to that car."

Dad couldn't run very well with all those tin cans lumping in his pockets. Ray easily would have won the race to the car if he hadn't slowed down and turned to wave at Grandma at her window. Grandpa was there, too. They both waved back.

When Dad got to the car, he pulled out the tin cans and threw them on the front seat, then started brushing himself all over with his hand. Ray brushed himself off, too. But Dad wasn't satisfied. He reached into the glove compartment and got out a little whisk broom. They took turns brushing each other. Dad took Ray's hat and looked it over carefully. "It looks all right," he decided. "Do I look all right?"

Ray nodded.

"Well, then remember. This is our secret about the bull and the hat."

Ray nodded again and hastily got in the car. It was urgent now to get home as fast as possible. He sat on the edge of the seat and leaned toward the windshield as if to help the car on. He held his hat on his lap, and kept one hand on the tin cans between him and Dad. Dad said it was a secret. But it wasn't only one secret he had with Dad, it was two, because if you gave the one away, the other would come out. It was two, and the secret about the hat was just as important as the secret about the bull. Then besides the two secrets he had with Dad, it still had to be kept secret from Martin that Dad knew about the tin cans. He hadn't told and tattled, but Martin would never believe he hadn't told Dad, and Martin had said he would scalp him if he told about the tin cans. Three secrets to keep! Of course, then there was still his very own secret—the secret plan to follow Shirley and Martin to the skunk hole.

Four secrets to keep! But he never could keep the secret about the tin cans if he and Dad didn't get home before Martin and Shirley and Mother. He sighed with relief when they turned up the yard, and he saw that the other car wasn't there. He put on his hat, picked up the cans, and he was out of the car almost before it stopped at the kitchen door. He ran to the garage.

In the stable he put all the boxes back exactly as they had been before Dad had moved them. He put the three cans back between the boxes exactly as they had been before, too, the kippered-herring one on the bottom. Then he stood, proud of himself.

He took off his hat and looked at it, and fanned himself with it the way Grandpa had done. Suddenly he felt his head. Martin had said he would scalp him, but Martin couldn't scalp him—he had a crew cut just like Martin's! He'd never thought, but, oh, it was good to think of it now. . . . The hat in his hand, he hopscotched out of the garage and over the yard, singsonging and chanting inside of himself, "Ha-ha, Martin can't scalp me. Ha-ha, Martin."

It was a wonderful relief that the three tin cans were back in place. Everything had turned out wonderfully well. And he knew four secrets! Thinking of that as he went hopscotch-

ing along to the kitchen door, he chanted
within himself, "Ha-ha, Martin, ha-ha, Shirley,
I know four secrets—and two secrets with my
Dad—and you don't." Then he hurried into the
house to be with his dad.

CHAPTER 5 * CLICK - CLOCK

After the long sleep that was Sunday night, it was Monday, it was school day, it was the day of the big plan to follow Martin and Shirley down the lane to watch what they did at the skunk hole. When Ray came down into the kitchen, everybody said, "Well, good morning, sleepyhead."

Shirley said it must be nice not to have to go to school, and not to have to get washed and dressed, and hurry up and eat breakfast. Shirley and Martin were all dressed, and they'd started their breakfast. Dad was in and out of the kitchen getting last-minute ready for taking the car out of town and being a salesman all week in faraway towns and places. Mother sat

62

on the edge of her chair sipping quick, nervous sips of her coffee. "Well, what a big, sleepy silence from you after our whole chorus of good mornings," she said. "I've been waiting for you. I've got a big washing to do, but I'm not going down in that mousy basement alone. It reeks of mice!"

"You can smell them way up here," Shirley said.

"Aw, girls!" Martin said. "Girls are all scared of mice."

"Well, Martin," Mother said, "thank you for including me among the girls, because I'm just as scared as Shirley. But I've got to go down in that basement while you sit in a nice, clean school."

"There's mice in the school," Ray said before he thought.

Dad squeezing past in the crowded kitchen back of Martin's chair gave Ray a look, because he'd almost given their secret away. It was hard to hold so many secrets! Ray felt really bad, but behind Shirley and Martin Dad made a great big wink and grinned at Ray. Then Ray quickly told Martin and everybody, "Girls, and ladies like Mother, are afraid of mice because they run up their legs." He asked Dad, "Why do mice run up girls' and ladies' legs, but not up boys' legs?"

"*Well!*" Mother said. "This certainly is a fitting subject just before I have to go in that basement with the mice. But that's a boy for you. Wakes up thinking and talking of mice —and digs into his breakfast."

But Ray asked again, "Why do they, Dad?"

"Why do they do what?" Dad said.

"Mice," Ray said. "Run up . . ."

Over Shirley's shoulder Dad gave Ray a warning shake of the head and made a nudge toward Mother. Then he said, "Now why don't you ask me an easy question, like, What was the name of Columbus's flagship?" He winked at Ray, and said loudly, "Guess before I go on my way with the car, I'd better repile those boxes in the horse stable."

Martin sat up with a jerk, but Shirley didn't catch on. She said, "I know the name of all of Columbus's ships! The . . ."

Behind her, Dad laid his hand over her mouth. "You ought to know," he said. "But I want Ray to tell me."

"The Nina, the Pinta, and the Santa Maria," Ray promptly said.

Shirley gasped in surprise behind Dad's hand. But Martin, who had told Ray the names of the ships, gave Ray a mean, dirty look, because now he knew Ray had tattled, and had told Dad about the tin cans. Martin made the silent word—tattletale—and then curled his lip. Ray looked at Dad. He wished Dad wouldn't give things away just to be teasing.

Dad caught on, and immediately said, "Well, got to run. I'll repile those boxes some other day." He went around the table kissing everyone good-bye, but Martin ducked his head under the table. Everybody laughed, and Martin wasn't mad anymore, because Dad wasn't going to repack the boxes so he wouldn't find the tin cans.

At the door Dad said, "Go down to the basement with Mother and stay there with her while she washes, won't you, Ray?"

Mother looked at him, so Ray had to promise Dad right there, and away went the plan for following Martin and Shirley down the lane. Dad left. Now Martin and Shirley dawdled over their breakfast. Ray knew just why. They were waiting until Mother was in the basement so they could sneak the tin cans out of the garage without being seen. Mother got up, and said, "Well, Raimie, let's go down to our stony, mousy dungeon. I'd just as soon get down there while Martin and Shirley are still home, and there's still some life up here in the kitchen."

Ray went ahead of Mother down the steep, narrow basement stairs. Mother came with the high-piled wash basket. She looked doubtfully over it down into the basement. "Gah," she said, "it reeks of mice."

In the kitchen Shirley yelled, "I can smell them up here." She jumped up, and slammed the cellar door shut.

"Well, thanks!" Mother said loudly through the closed door. "I only hope the school is full of mice, and they run all over your feet."

Ray knew that Shirley had slammed the door shut because she and Martin wanted to run out to the garage to get the tin cans. Mother suddenly said, "Ray, how did you know there are mice in the school?" But then she said to herself, "Well, even I can't get off the subject of mice! But never mind, I'll feel better once I've got the washing machine started, and hear its homely old sounds."

Ray told Mother, "Mice don't run up boys' legs, because boys wear trousers."

Mother set the wash basket down. "Well, you're bright this morning. First all the names of those ships, and now—why didn't I think of that? Trousers! I'm running right up right now to put on slacks." Then she changed her mind. "No, I'll get the washing machine started first."

While Mother filled the washing machine a piece of mortar fell from between the big, round field stones in the basement wall, and shattered on the floor. Mother jumped, and actually squeaked. Ray laughed at her. "You're the one sounds like a mouse!"

"Don't stand there laughing," Mother said nervously. "I know I'm foolishly afraid of mice. I admit it. Just keep talking to me until I've got the old washing machine stamping and pounding."

It was hard to start talking when somebody just said: "Start talking." All of a sudden there wasn't a thing Ray could think to talk about—except mice. He thought about the skunk, because his big plan of following Martin and Shirley had gone all wrong, but he certainly couldn't talk to Mother about skunks. He thought about the bull and the awfulness of yesterday. . . . Then at last he thought to say,

67

"Dad says we're going to have a whole new basement with new, solid concrete walls. Dad says in the old days when they built this house, they rolled the stones out of the fields, and made them into any kind of a rough, old basement wall. They just plastered mortar between the stones, and then slapped whitewash and plaster over it all with a brush."

Mother looked around at the big stones and the dirty, gray mortar between them. "Don't you on Monday morning tell me your dad's big Sunday plans," she said disgustedly. "I suppose he's just going to change this basement some easy Saturday afternoon!" She looked up at the tiny, cobwebby basement window, and started the washing machine. It began to pound and rock and make slamming, stamping sounds.

Mother stepped back from the washing machine, hands on her hips. "Look at it!" she shouted over the noise. "This old dirt floor is so lumpy and bumpy that machine never stands on all its four legs at once, and never on the same three. This miserable house has a miserable dirt-floor basement where I'm surrounded by stones and by mice, and chased by a washing machine! I could scream! Now why do you stand there so quiet?"

"But Dad is going to put in new walls," Ray told her, surprised. "And, Mother, you know Grandpa's old fallen-down shed? Dad's going to put it up for Grandpa—for Grandpa's horse."

Suddenly Mother wasn't angry anymore. She came around the washing machine, dropped to one knee, and held Ray. "Sure he is, Raimie," she said. "He's going to put in new basement walls, and he's going to set up the shed. Dad believes that, and you believe it, and I do, too."

There was a hard slam above them, and plaster and mortar rattled down the wall. Mother jumped. "What was that?"

Shirley and Martin must have run out of the house, and in their hurry they'd slammed the kitchen door too hard.

"Was that Shirley and Martin?" Mother asked.

Woefully Ray nodded. Shirley and Martin were gone, and now his deep, secret plan of following them was gone, too.

"With them gone," Mother said hurriedly, "I'm going to run up and put on slacks. If it's because of long trousers boys aren't afraid of mice, I've got to try trousers. Want to come along?"

Ray shook his head. Maybe with Mother

69

changing to slacks in her bedroom upstairs, he could run out, just to the head of the lane, and still watch Martin and Shirley.

The next moment Mother called from the kitchen, "Oh, Raimie—Shirley and Martin left their apples. I'd laid them out on the counter. I do like them to have an apple with their school lunch. Could you run after them? I seem to hear them yelling in the lane."

There it suddenly was—the whole plan springing back into place—and now he could run out with Mother's permission! He raced up the stairs. Mother handed him the two apples and opened the door for him. "Hear?" she said. "They're still in the lane, yelling like a couple of wild Indians."

Way down the lane Shirley had run past the skunk hole. Ray could see the cornstalks poking up from it. But even though Shirley was past, she kept screaming. Her head was thrown back, and her hair was flying.

Martin was waiting this side of the poking sticks. He still had to rattle them, and yell down the skunk hole. Ray ran up the lane so he could really see Martin. Martin began running, but he couldn't run fast. He had to run by just sort of wriggling his shoulders because he had the three tin cans in his pockets and they kept popping out. Martin had to hold his hands over them. Ray, running silently after Martin, was even catching up with him.

Martin did not run screaming like Shirley. Martin even dared come to a complete stop at the skunk hole. He grabbed the cornstalks and really shook them. Then Martin bent down with his face right over the hole, and yelled, "You dirty old skunk down there. Who's afraid of you? Yah, you! You stink."

Martin ran to catch up with Shirley. Shirley didn't wait. She climbed the lane fence, jumped over into the cornfield, and was gone in the corn. Martin almost flew up the fence, grabbed the top of a fence post, and sailed himself over. He lost a tin can, turned, picked it up, and charged away into the corn after Shirley.

Suddenly Ray was alone in the lane, right near the skunk hole. It was still. He stood petrified. He was alone. He wanted to turn and run back home, but that wasn't right either. He still had to call to Martin and Shirley about the apples. "Mar—tin, Shirl—eeee. You forgot your apples." But he couldn't seem to call it out. He began to cry, and then he was screaming out Martin's and Shirley's names. Suddenly he dropped both apples and ran.

Behind him Martin and Shirley came bursting out of the corn. "I saw you," Shirley yelled. "You didn't think, but . . . Martin! The little sneak was spying on us!"

Martin was so angry he came over the fence. He grabbed Ray by the hand and ran with him to the start of the lane. Martin stopped behind the broken-down apple tree to keep out of Mother's sight, then he said, "What's the matter with you, following us? You know you're not supposed to follow us. And you tattled to Dad about our tin cans, didn't you? Thought you were so smart about their names!"

Shirley had run along with them on the other side of the fence. Now she said loudly, "You're a crybaby and a scared baby, but that's what you get for following us! And you'd better not tell Mother. Gee whiz, Martin! Now we can't even sail our boats anymore—all because of him! We're so late now we've got to run all the way to school."

"If you do it again," Martin threatened,

"tattle and follow us, I'll . . . I'll scalp you, and I don't care if you have got a crew cut, I'll cut your head off at the neck. Now get in the house!"

"Come on, Martin, hurry!" Shirley yelled.

Martin climbed the fence. In a moment he and Shirley were gone down the corn rows. "I didn't either," Ray sobbed after them. "Mother sent me. You forgot your . . ." Suddenly he felt mean and angry, too. Just as mean as Martin and Shirley had been to him. Just because they were big school kids! He didn't call out to them about the apples. Anyway, he'd dropped them. He hoped the skunk would eat them. He didn't care.

But the two big red apples still lay in the lane near the skunk hole. Mother would ask, "Did you give Shirley and Martin the apples?" Then what would he say? He couldn't tell Mother he had thrown Shirley's and Martin's apples away.

Indignant and wrathful he peered under the apple tree and saw a big stick. He picked it up. Clutching his big stick he started back up the lane after the apples. There wasn't a skunk. Dad had said so. And it wasn't a skunk hole.

73

Dad had said it was an old, empty woodchuck den. Shirley and Martin didn't even know that! He stopped to yell it out into the cornfield. "Ha-ha. There isn't even a skunk down in there. Dad said so. He said you were silly. Ha-ha, Martin. Ha-ha, Shirley. SILLY!"

Nobody answered. The corn rustled in a little breeze, then there was silence. Everything stood still and seemed to listen and wait. Ray didn't call out anymore. He clutched the stick and eyed the silent skunk hole. There wasn't a skunk down there. Dad had said so! Suddenly he wasn't so sure. Dad had gone out of town. Shirley and Martin had gone. It was awfully lonely and still. And there lay the apples.

Way up the lane there was a cheery whistle. Another whistle answered the first whistle almost from right behind Ray. For a moment he was sure it was Shirley and Martin, but then a bird flew to the top of the fence post. It was a bobwhite. It whistled "bobwhite." Then another bobwhite flew to the top of the fence post above the skunk hole.

It wasn't nearly so scary anymore with a bobwhite whistling a cheery little whistle right above the skunk hole. Ray puckered his lips

74

and tried to whistle "bobwhite" too. After about five tries he managed it. Amazingly the near bobwhite answered him, and the bobwhite way up the lane answered *him*. With the bobwhite whistling on top of the fence post above the skunk hole, Ray stole up to the apples, but he kept a tight hold on his big stick.

Suddenly it came to him. Suddenly he knew just what to do to get the apples back from near the skunk hole! When he'd been very little, and Shirley had had to take care of him, Shirley quite often would take a stick and draw a square around him with the point of the stick. She would tell him he was locked inside the square and couldn't get out. He was so little then, he'd believed her, and he'd never tried to crawl out of the square. Shirley used to chant a little song when she marked out the square all around him. How did it go again? Ray tried hard to remember. But he'd been so little then, he couldn't remember it all. He had to make some of it up himself—but now he said it right out to the bobwhite on the fence post.

> "*Click-clock,*
> *Turn the lock.*

Shut the window,
Close the door.
And click-clock,
Turn the lock,
And nothing can get in."

All the time he made up the song he marked out a square with the big stick. Now he could reach out with the stick and pull the apples inside of his square. He picked up the apples, but he kept his eye on the skunk hole as he stooped to pick them up. Then suddenly, for no reason at all, he took one of the apples and rolled it up against the cornstalks that poked up out of the skunk hole. That was for the skunk—if there was a skunk there. He turned and ran hard down the lane with the other apple.

When he got back to the broken-down apple tree he pushed the big stick under it and hid the apple under the tree. He was proud of himself. He'd treated the skunk with respect—just as Dad had said he should do. He hadn't shouted any mean things down the hole to the skunk, and he'd even left him an apple.

Mother opened the kitchen door as Ray came across the yard. Mother had slacks on. She'd

76

even put rubber bands around the bottoms of the legs of the slacks. She laughed at herself. "The silly tricks you pull," she said. "I don't believe that mice run up your legs, but it helped to put on slacks and rubber bands. Now the mice can't, even though they don't. Well, ready to go down in the dungeon again, now that you're back from school? By now that washing machine must be climbing the walls."

"School?" Ray said.

"Yes, you must have followed Shirley and Martin all the way to school, you were gone so long."

"Oh, no, Mother. I didn't even give Martin and Shirley the apples. I . . . I played in the lane."

"Played school?" Mother asked. "Else what did you do with the apples?"

He didn't understand. "But I don't know how to play school," he said.

"Never mind—just a joke," Mother said. "Let's get down to that basement."

The washing machine had moved, but of course it hadn't climbed up the walls. It was making great slamming noises and shaking the soap suds out of itself from under the lid.

"If we'd set the casters in something," Mother said, "maybe the washing machine wouldn't move around so. See if you can find some old rubbers or galoshes under the stairs. There are boxes there that haven't even been unpacked yet from the moving."

Ray ducked in under the old basement stairway. He was hardly there when Mother called, "Did you find anything?" She sounded scared. Suddenly Ray thought of the click-clock square, and then he knew just what to do. He didn't look for rubbers; he found a stick. He ran back to Mother with the stick and traced a square in the lumpy dirt floor around Mother and the washing machine. She stood there and looked down at it, puzzled. But Ray chanted the song while he made the square:

> *"Click-clock,*
> *Turn the lock.*
> *Shut the window,*
> *Close the door.*
> *And click-clock,*
> *Turn the lock,*
> *And nothing can get in."*

"Nothing, hunh?" Mother said. "Just like

that nothing can get at me. No mice, nothing. How do the mice know?"

"They don't know—you know," Ray said impatiently. "And he won't let."

"Who won't let?"

"God won't let," he said.

Mother gasped. "Is that a game that you made up?"

He nodded.

"But when do you play the click-clock game?"

"When I'm scared," he said.

"Were you scared in the lane?" Mother asked. "I could see you'd been crying."

Oh, his mother was wonderful. She had seen that he'd cried, but she'd made believe she hadn't noticed anything. "I was at first," he told Mother. "But then I played the click-clock game, and then I wasn't afraid."

"But, Ray," Mother said. "Think. When you mark a square like that around you and you feel safe, you aren't really safe, are you? I mean—what if a fierce dog came? The dog wouldn't stop for a line you'd traced in the dirt, now would he? I mean, it's wonderful, Ray, but I don't want you to depend on it too much."

"Oh, no, Mother!"

"Yes, but if a fierce dog came, what would you do?"

"I don't know any fierce dogs, Mother. But if a fierce, awful bull would come, you mustn't sit still in your square. You must run and jump and zigzag, and climb over a fence as fast as you can, because a bull can't come over a fence."

"I'm glad to know that," Mother said. "I had to know that you just wouldn't sit there making yourself believe you were safe. And now I think I know. Making the square doesn't lock you in. It locks your scaredness out; it's the scaredness can't come in! That's it, isn't it?"

He looked up at his mother, open-mouthed. He nodded his head, and stepped in the square to be near her. She had made it all clear! Softly he said, "Yes, Mother."

"It's the same idea as my putting on slacks —so that mice that don't run up legs, can't run up my legs. It helps, doesn't it? And so does tracing the square. Well, then, just to show you I believe in it, too, go find something for the washing machine casters, and I'll wait inside your square."

All he could find in the boxes under the

spidery stair were a pair of rubbers and a pair of galoshes. He went back to the washing machine with them, but before he stepped into the square he chanted: "Click-clock, door unlock." Then he stepped inside the square. Mother lifted each separate leg of the washing machine off the ground while he slid a rubber or a galosh under the casters. There stood the washing machine, and now it looked as if it were walking away. But now it really stood still. And it wasn't half so noisy.

Mother said, "My, what a silly sight. A washing machine wearing galoshes!" She stepped back to look at it, but remembered just in time. "Click-clock, door unlock," she said, before she stepped out of the square.

"Mother," Ray asked, "now are you scared anymore?"

When he asked that, Mother suddenly kneeled on the lumpy floor in front of him. "Ray," she said, "just because I am a 'fraidy cat, I mustn't let myself make a scared baby out of you, must I? I must let you go down the lane alone and play your all-alone games."

"Mom," he said earnestly, "I want to play that going-to-school game of yours in the lane."

82

"*My* going to school game?" Mother said, puzzled.

"Yes," he said, "make believe I go to school in the lane."

"Oh," Mother said uncertainly. "All right. Then when you come home from school—just as with Shirley and Martin—I'll have a glass of chocolate milk and a piece of cake waiting for you. But, Ray, it won't spoil your school game if I go up in the attic and look for you out of the high window sometimes? From that high attic window I can just see your head moving along the lane in between the tall corn."

"May I take an apple to school, too—just like Shirley and Martin?" he asked.

"An apple and a lollipop," Mother promised cheerfully, "every day you go to your make-believe school. And you can go every day, except when it rains."

He stared at his mother. She had invented a game for him. She had made up the school-going game the way he had made up the click-clock game.

"You won't mind then," Mother asked, "that you can't go to school for another year? You and your Nina and Pinta and Santa Maria. Smarty!"

83

Oh, his mother was wonderful to have thought of the school game. He hugged her. Then Mother got up from the lumpy floor that was hurting her knees, and said, "Come up to the attic with me. I want to show you how I can see you down in the lane."

They went up to the attic. They stood together at the attic window. As far as the eye could see there went the corn over the hills and down in the valleys. There was the lane deep as a canal between the tall corn. Why, there were the bobwhites again, flying from fence post to fence post.

Mother said, "I should have brought up some of the wash suds to clean this window. You can hardly see through it." But then she shoved up the bottom sash. They both kneeled on the attic floor and leaned out of the window.

"Isn't it beautiful, Raimie?" Mother said. "Isn't it beautiful? The corn going down in the valleys and up over the hills?" She murmured a poem from the Bible softly to herself. Ray could hear the murmuring words. They were as beautiful as the words that were the names of the ships of Columbus—Nina and Pinta and Santa Maria. He pressed his head against her side, "Say it again, Mother."

She said it again for him, slowly:

"The little hills rejoice on every side.
The pastures are clothed with flocks;
The valleys are covered over with corn;
They shout for joy, they also sing."

The words were in his ears, going into his mind. They tucked themselves away there. Mother got up. "Now," she said quietly, "you run down to the kitchen, grab an apple and a lollipop, and go and play in the lane. Run, boy!"

"But what about the washing?" he asked.

"Oh, I'm going down to finish the washing."

"Alone?" he asked, astounded.

"Didn't you make a square for me? I'll just go click-clock. I won't be afraid inside my square."

"Oh, yes," he said, delighted. "Say it again about the little hills that shout for joy and sing also," he urged. But he couldn't wait. He stormed down the stairs.

CHAPTER 6 * THE END
OF THE LANE

Ray picked up the apple and the big stick he had left under the broken-down apple tree. It was hard to stoop. In the kitchen he had shoved three lollipops in one pocket, and a big apple— the biggest one in the bag—in his other pocket. Now the apple from under the tree still had to go on top of that apple. The lollipop sticks stuck out of one pocket, the two apples bulged in the other pocket and made everything tight, but carrying the stick he walked stoutly on to the skunk hole.

Then he saw there was a cock pheasant there.

86

The pheasant was pecking at the apple he had rolled to the hole for the skunk. The pheasant's neck bobbed and flashed with colors as he pecked away at the apple. With the pheasant there, it wasn't scary at all.

Before Ray got near, the pheasant ducked his neck and skulked away into the corn. As if they'd been waiting for that, the bobwhites flew to two different fence posts, and began whistling. It wasn't scary at all at the skunk hole.

Ray curiously picked up the apple. It was full of small, round holes from the pheasant's pecking. Ray wondered if bobwhites liked apples, too. He even dared to climb the fence and lay the apple on top of the skunk hole post. He quickly climbed down again, and picked up the stick. As he stooped to pick up the stick, he said in his nicest voice toward the hole to the skunk that wasn't there, "You're a nice skunk." He hopscotched on up the lane proud of himself because he had dared, and hadn't forgotten to treat the skunk with respect the way Dad had said. It hurt a little to hopscotch, the apples bulged so hard and tight. He had to keep his free hand over the lollipop sticks. The bobwhites kept fluttering ahead from fence post to fence post, then one flew around and behind Ray and one stayed ahead. Now he was between the bobwhites and between their whistles. He decided that right there was a good place to play the school game.

He traced a big square in the dirt of the lane with the point of the stick. Not a click-clock square; it had to be much bigger to be a schoolroom. Inside the big square he drew all kinds of little squares. They were the desks and seats. In one corner of the square he drew the oval table full of little circles. Those were the dishpans. The bobwhites whistled, but he was tracing so hard, tongue pressed between his lips, he didn't have time to answer them. But the moment he was finished with the oval table he said to the bobwhites, "My name is Ray Garroway—not Bob White."

It wasn't very funny, but just the same it was a nice little joke to have with the bobwhites here in the quiet country. The corn rustled in a little wind. The rustling went into sighing. He looked around to whistle to the bobwhites, but they were gone. He stepped into the big square and sat down on the ground inside one of the little squares that was a desk and seat.

It was done. All of a sudden there was nothing to do, nothing but sit on the ground in the stillness under the sighing that went through the high corn tassels. He pulled one of the lollipops out of his pocket, but he didn't know whether he could sit licking a lollipop in school—he thought maybe just in the lunch hour. He pushed the lollipop back in his pocket.

And there, suddenly, the whole school game died. All you could do in the school game was sit. And when you sat way down on the ground with the corn rising all around you everything was so still.

The game was no good! Mother had thought it up, but the game was no good. Maybe all-alone games weren't any good, unless you made them up for yourself. He didn't know enough about school to know what to do in the school game. Anyway, it wasn't a school anymore. It was just scratches in the dirt. He sat in the stillness. The corn did not sigh anymore; the wind had died in the corn. Three black crows flapped out of the sky, the bobwhites hadn't come back —all was still. Everything seemed to be waiting.

He thought of jumping up and running

home to ask Mother how to play the school game. He looked down the lane, but he stayed in the square. He was scared in the stillness. He didn't dare run back past the skunk hole. He listened to the stillness.

It wasn't so! Little hills did not shout for joy and sing also. Of course, there were no hills here. And when he'd gone down the creek with Dad yesterday, he hadn't listened to the little hills, because he hadn't known. Maybe you couldn't listen except all alone. But when you were all alone the stillness got scary.

He couldn't sit still anymore. He had to run out of his school—it was just some scratches in the dirt anyway. He ran hard, pounding hard, up the long lane.

Way up the lane he came to a spot where a tractor had turned out of the cornfield into the lane. Now the dirt was hard and dusty and dry, but when the tractor had gone up the lane the ground must have been wet and muddy because the tractor had made two deep tracks. Now, hard and dry, the two tractor tracks still went up the lane.

Suddenly there was a game! A loud, hard, noisy game! He jumped down into one of the tractor ruts, feet tight together. He shuff-shuffed his feet back and forth to get under motion, to get up power and steam. With his shuff-shuffing feet puffing up dust in the rut, just like that he'd become a train. He was a train! He was a big, long freight train that went way back to the skunk hole. He was the big engine.

Everything everywhere would be able to hear him come; everything that was listening. And everything had better clear the track, because a train couldn't watch out; a train could only keep coming.

He listened to the shuff-shuffing noises around his feet. The dust was puffing up around them in spurts like the steam around the wheels of a real locomotive. Then from the power in his shuffing feet the hiss of steam began to come from between his clenched teeth.

The big train came into motion. He wailed a long, loud wail, and then a still longer wail to warn everything that the train was coming. He bent his neck and lowered his head with the power. Even the apples tight in his pocket helped the feeling of power. He chug-achugged and his feet puffed dust. His hands pistoned powerfully back and forth. He kept his head down—a train didn't have to look ahead. Everything had to look out and get out of the way of a train. He wailed his warning wail, and on came the train up the long lane.

The train kept chugging up the tractor track that kept going up the lane. But then the train was not only going up the lane. It started going up a hill! Here was a hill! The powerful train had to chug hard to get all that long, endless string of box cars up the hill. He bowed his neck with the pull and the power.

Up the rise of the hill the tractor rut got shallower and shallower. Then halfway up the hill there was no more track. The train had to stop. The train stopped. Ray looked up, because he had become a boy again. There was a fence halfway up the hill. It went all around the top of the sharp little hill. There was a gate in the fence. The lane ended at the gate in the fence. Here was the end of the lane. But a horse was standing on the tippety-top of the hill, looking down at Ray. A big white horse! The horse whinnied at Ray. Suddenly the horse came plunging down the hill straight at the gate and Ray.

The horse came pounding the way the bull had pounded over the ground, and as with the bull, Ray turned to stone. He couldn't run, he couldn't move. And then the horse hit the gate. He pressed so hard against the gate with his big white chest the top of the gate tipped and tilted down. It screaked and squealed against the chain that held it tied to the fence post.

The gate was going to crash down, and then the horse would come right over it! Ray turned to run. Right behind him the horse neighed a long neigh. It squealed out over the fields. Ray's legs wouldn't run. He cried out with helplessness. He desperately looked back. The gate hadn't come down. It held against the push of the horse, and the horse nickered at him. Ray said, "Hi, nice horse," in his nicest voice, but it came out a tiny, soft whisper. He cleared his throat and tried again. "Hi, horse."

The horse heard. He tossed his head up, and tossed his tail up, and switched himself hard with his tail. He swished and swished his tail, and that made it look as if he was glad that Ray had said "Hi" to him.

The big eyes of the horse stared at him. His chest pushed the gate. The gate screaked again. Ray had a quick, hopeful thought. "Do you want a sucker?" he asked the horse. "I've got an apple, too." He had a sudden, better thought —a quick, clever fib. "Oh, I forgot," he told the horse, "I left the apple down the lane. It was all pecked by a bird, but that won't hurt it any. Shall I go get it for you?"

The horse swished his broomy tail, and looked at Ray. The two big apples lumped hard in Ray's pocket. The horse looked as if he knew that Ray wasn't going to go get the pheasant-pecked apple but was going to run straight home. "I'll get it right now," he guiltily told the horse.

He turned to run. Behind him the chain rattled, the gate squeaked, and the horse nickered and nickered after him. It was a strange, lonely sound. It was something like an old man laughing. Maybe if he rolled an apple under the gate to the horse, while the horse was eating it he could quickly run away. He nervously began to work the apple out of his tight pocket. His fingers wouldn't work fast enough. He watched the horse. The horse watched him. The apple wouldn't come. Desperately Ray ran a few steps toward the gate and flung all his three lollipops over the gate to the horse.

94

The lollipops fell on the ground. The horse picked them up one by one with long, quivery lips. Then he crunched down on all three at once with his big, yellow teeth—sticks and all! He chewed and he slobbered and spilled wet crumbs, but he did not drop the sticks. He was eating the sucker sticks, too!

"You mustn't," Ray yelled at him. "Not the sticks! They're not good for you."

He stood in an agony as the horse crunched on.

Now the horse would die from eating the lollipop sticks. He'd eaten all three! He'd swallowed them, for now he was running his long lips over the ground hunting up the wet crumbs he had spilled.

Ray wanted to run, but he stayed rooted. Now the horse was going to die! That's what Martin had said. Long ago Martin had told him that if you swallowed a sucker stick it would pierce your stomach, and a couple days later it would come sticking out from between your ribs, and then you'd die. Shirley had said it was true. If you swallowed sucker sticks or chewing gum, you'd die. It must be so. Mother always warned him never to run with a sucker stick in his mouth, because it might go down his throat. All three sticks had gone down the horse's throat!

Suddenly he had a hopeful thought. What if he gave the horse the two apples? Apples were good for you! Maybe if the horse ate the apples he wouldn't die from the sucker sticks. He worked the apples out of his pocket. He rolled them under the gate. Then he ran, but he couldn't run away. He came back and hid in the corn. He hunched down in the corn rows and secretly watched the horse.

The horse had eaten the apples. Now the horse just stood there, head hanging over the gate. His head was so heavy the gate made little squeaky mouse sounds. Then in the awful, waiting stillness, the insides of the horse began to rumble. Now the horse was going to die! Ray scrunched deeper down in the corn, wretchedly watching the horse.

All of a sudden the horse pricked up his ears. He lifted his head, tossed his head, nickered and nickered, all excited, and trotted away along the fence. But he stopped again, leaned far over the fence, and neighed out over the cornfield. From the cornfield a faraway neighing answered him. Then another neighing from another direction. The horse stamped, and switched himself with his broomy tail.

There out of the corn, neighing and neighing, came Shirley and Martin. Shirley was first. She had her school lunch bucket with her. She went right up to the fence and petted the horse. She wasn't afraid of the horse! She rubbed his nose, and even his lips! Then Shirley ran with the lunch bucket to the gate. The horse wheeled around and ran after her on the other side of the fence. Shirley set the lunch bucket down, and climbed up the gate, even though the big horse was standing tight against it! Martin came running up, but from the top of the gate Shirley yelled at him. "It's my turn. You had the first ride Friday noon."

Just like that Shirley jumped from the top of the gate and let herself sort of fall onto the horse's back. She pushed herself up, sat straight, and said, "Giddyap, giddyap."

The old horse swished his tail, tossed his head, and galloped away with Shirley. He followed the fence around the hill. Martin climbed to the top of the gate to sit and watch.

Hunched down among the corn, Ray was so

excited he was almost afraid Martin would hear
him breathe. It was unbelievable. It was hard
not to run out to Martin and sit on the gate
with him and ask him all kinds of questions.
He couldn't, he mustn't. He had to stay hidden
and quiet, otherwise—just like this morning—
Martin and Shirley would think he was spying
on them. And then if they found out he had
given the horse sucker sticks! He hunched
down lower in the corn.

Now Shirley was coming back around the hill. The horse had taken her all around his pasture. He stopped at the gate. Shirley reached out, grabbed the top board of the gate, and pulled herself off the horse. She climbed down and went to her lunch bucket. She came back with a sandwich. She fed the sandwich to the horse! She let the horse eat it right out of her hand!

Martin had jumped on the horse, but now he waited for the horse to finish eating the sandwich. Then Martin said, "Okay, now take me around, and you'll get my sandwich, too. No apples today. We forgot our apples this morning."

Oh, it was secret! This must be Martin's and Shirley's real real secret. They had told him about playing Indian and hound-and-hare, and about sailing tin cans in the creek, but this was the real secret—that Shirley and Martin knew a horse, and rode the horse in their school lunch hour.

Now Martin was ready to take the horse around the pasture, but Shirley begged, "Let's both ride him. Come on, Martin. Let me get on behind you."

Martin said, "Naw, it's my turn. Anyway, we shouldn't both get on this poor old skinny horse. He's got nothing in his pasture to eat. He's eaten all his grass. Golly, Shirl, you can't expect him to take us both around on just a sandwich!"

Shirley didn't argue. "Martin," she said, "let's both ask Mother for an extra sandwich every day. Then we can each give the horse two sandwiches and an apple."

"Hey, that's a good idea," Martin said.

He was just going to start the horse, but Shirley said, "Martin, look! Sucker sticks here on the ground. Three of them!"

Martin looked down from the horse. "D'you suppose Rim's been here? D'you suppose he found out about the horse?"

"He wouldn't dare come way out here," Shirley said slowly, "he's too big a scared baby."

"Yeah," Martin said. "Must be some other kids are riding the horse on the sly, too. With no house around and nobody near anybody can ride him. But gosh, Shirl—Rim mustn't find out. He tells Mother everything."

"No," Shirley agreed. "So don't you go telling Ray. Not even when you're mad at me, the

100

way you did about sailing tin cans in the creek. Why, Mother would die if she knew we rode a horse. She'd just die!"

"Yeah," Martin said. "Boy, if I ever catch Rim sneaking around here!"

Scrunched down among the corn, Ray couldn't help himself. He had to cry a little, but it was for joy. The horse hadn't eaten the sucker sticks! He'd crunched the candy off the

sticks, and later he'd spat out the sticks. Oh, it was marvelous. He felt soft with relief.

"Oh, Martin," Shirley was saying, "we've got to get back to school. I'll race you on your old horse. Bet I can run faster!"

Martin slapped the horse on the rump. He spanked and spanked the poor old horse. But Shirley ran faster. She ran past the horse, then the horse began to run after Shirley.

Oh, it was exciting. Ray could hardly tear himself away from his secret watching, but now that Shirley and Martin were going away from him he had to get down the lane as fast as he could. If they caught him spying on them again! He crept down the corn row, then ran hard down the lane.

In the kitchen a glass of chocolate milk and a piece of cake—just as Mother had promised, and just as big as Shirley's and Martin's—were waiting for him. Mother came hurrying into the kitchen. "Was it a good game, Raimie? It must have been, you played so long. Why, here it's almost one o'clock!"

"Oh, Mother, I had fun," he said. "I played school and I played train, and . . . "

"Well, then I'm glad I thought of such a good game for you," Mother said.

Oh, but the cake and chocolate milk were good! It was just as if he were adding the cake and the chocolate milk on top of the big, exciting secret he knew about the horse. Martin and Shirley didn't even know that he knew! Now he was going to run out every day, and every day he'd give the horse an apple and a lollipop —but without the stick. He'd even climb to the top of the gate, and sit there and talk to the horse the way Martin and Shirley did. He'd talk to the horse and tell the horse everything. Why, then he wouldn't have to keep his secrets alone anymore! He bit into the cake, and with his mouth full asked Mother, "Can I play school in the lane again this afternoon?"

"May I," Mother said.

"May I?" he said obediently.

"I'll have to see about this afternoon," Mother said. "But you surely may every day that it doesn't rain. Later, of course—this is fall —it will get too wet and too cold."

But that seemed so far away. He bit into his cake—a great big bite.

CHAPTER 7 * THE HORSE
ON THE HILL

Shirley hadn't thought of it, Martin hadn't
thought of it. Only he—Ray! He thought of it
in the middle of the night. In the night the
moon had come out. The moonlight in his
room had awakened Ray. But he'd awakened
glad, not scared. Glad that he'd found the horse,
and glad the horse hadn't eaten the lollipop
sticks and hadn't died.

It was such a good thought to wake up with
he'd had to get out of bed and run to the
window to see if in the moonlight he could see
the horse on the faraway hill. All he could see

104

was the corn, but he'd imagined he could see the hill in the moonlight, and the white horse standing white in the moonlight. He'd pictured the horse standing there sleeping with head hanging down, because horses could stand on their four legs and sleep. That's what Martin had said!

It had been nice to stand in the night at the window and imagine things. Then suddenly it had come to him—the happy, wide-awake thought. The horse's hill was the little hill that shouted for joy and also sang! For here up in his room, although he had to be mouse quiet because he was out of his bed, inside *he* was shouting and singing for joy, because he knew the horse. That must be the way little hills shouted and sang!

The moonlit sky was hurrying with clouds. The night was white and still and secret. Right then he thought of it! He'd feed the horse corn!

Martin and Shirley hadn't thought of feeding the horse corn. They'd pulled up all kinds of cornstalks for sticks to push down into the skunk hole, but they hadn't thought of pulling up corn for the poor skinny old horse. All they gave him was a sandwich, and for that the horse

105

had to give them a ride! But what was a sand-wich for a big horse?

In his mind, at the night window, Ray could picture the whole, round, hilltop pasture. The grass all over the hill was clipped short. The horse had eaten all the grass.

Why, of course! That was why there was a path all around the outside of the horse's pasture where no corn grew. After eating all the grass the horse had pushed his head and neck out through the barbed-wire fence, and had eaten all the corn he could reach.

Only beyond the fence posts were there still two or three or four stalks of corn left standing. He had noticed it yesterday. Now he knew why. The horse couldn't push out the barbed wire far enough to reach those stalks of corn growing beyond the fence posts. There, just like that, came the marvelous plan. He'd pull up the corn still standing at every post, and feed it to the horse. Oh, now he could really shout and sing! He had thought of it in the night. In the morning he'd do it! He raced back to bed and jumped in—as if to help make the morning come faster.

It was hard to believe he'd slept way too long

after his wonderful plan in the night. He ran down the stairs. There was no one in the kitchen but Mother. Shirley and Martin had already gone to school. Mother looked at him and said, "What a happy boy! What are you bubbling about?"

But he asked, "Mom, today can I—I mean, may I—have two apples and two lollipops? And may I play in the lane right after breakfast?"

Mother just laughed, and gave him a kiss.

He hastily told her he was hungry, and then said again, "May I, Mother?"

Mother said, "Not a crumb for breakfast, and not even one apple for your school game. Nothing faces you but pure starvation, unless you kiss me back."

So he kissed her, sat down at the table, and asked, "Have Martin and Shirley gone to school already?"

"Yes," Mother said. "And for once decently by road. One of our new neighbors picked them up in his car. They'll be coming back by road, too, because they want to stop at a little country store and pick up kippered herring and sardines. Imagine. One of their new school friends—they must be Scots—have kippered herring for breakfast. Now Shirley and Martin

107

want kippered herring for their breakfast every morning. And smelly sardine sandwiches in their lunch!" Mother made a face. "I don't know how I'm going to stand the smell of hot kippered herring the first thing in the morning, but at least you and I won't have to eat them."

"Oh," Ray said, "I'll eat them all right."

He couldn't tell Mother, but it must mean that Martin and Shirley had lost their tin cans and needed now Ninas and Pintas and Santa Marias. And if they sailed boats, maybe they wouldn't ride the poor old skinny horse. Oh, he was very willing to help Shirley and Martin get empty cans. He told Mother again, "I'll eat kippered herring for breakfast. And, Mom, can I have sardine sandwiches, too, at noon?"

Mother made an awful face. "You, too, Raimie! I still had a can of herring in the house for this morning, and there's a piece left in the can, but I'm not heating kippered herring again. It was sickening enough this morning."

Ray told Mother he would eat it cold.

"All right," she said, "if you've got to do everything that Martin and Shirley do."

It tasted funny after orange juice and sweet cereal and chocolate milk, but he ate the piece

108

of kippered herring without making a face. It all helped to make boats to sail in the creek.

Mother watched him. "Don't bolt so," she said. "There's no hurry."

She didn't know!

This time when Ray got to the hilltop pasture, the horse was at the gate waiting for him. He had his head over the gate, and nickered and neighed at Ray.

Ray breathlessly told the horse, "Mother let me go right after breakfast, and she gave me two apples and two lollipops, but I'm going to feed you corn."

He almost reached for an apple, but right now there wasn't even time for that. He was quaky inside with eagerness to try out his wonderful plan. He hurried along the fence, and the horse promptly followed him on his side of the fence. The horse swung along, swinging and swishing his tail. Ray explained it all. "After the corn we'll eat the apples and the lollipops. I've got two of each, but Mother would hardly give them to me." He laughed. "Do you know what she said? She said two apples might easily give me a stomach ache, and

109

you couldn't sit in school with a stomach ache."

It was just as if the horse understood, for he suddenly poked his head between the strands of barbed wire and nuzzled his long lips over Ray's pocket. As if he knew the apples were there! Ray twisted away, then without thinking, he just pushed the horse's head away from his pocket. "You mustn't slobber so," he told the horse.

The horse jerked his head back through the fence. Ray looked up at him. There were tears running down the horse's long face! It was a sorry thing to see a big horse cry tears because you had pushed his head away. Ray was ashamed. "I didn't mean it that way," he explained.

He was so sorry, he pulled out one of the apples and rolled it under the fence to the horse. The horse grabbled it up with quivering lips. He crunched and he munched, and it suddenly seemed it would be a wonderful thing not only to talk to the horse but to eat with the horse. Ray took out a lollipop. He licked on the lollipop while the horse ate the apple.

But the horse saw—quickly swallowed the apple, and reached out through the fence for

110

the lollipop Ray was licking. He tried to grab it. He wanted it so badly Ray held out the lollipop to him. Suddenly he thought of the stick, then scary as it was, he had to hang on. The horse neatly pulled the round ball of candy off the end of the stick, and Ray held onto it. The horse crunched and munched and spilled. Oh, but it was exciting now. Why, he'd fed the big horse right out of his hand—almost the way Shirley did! He thrilled with pride; he threw the stick hard, threw it as far away into the cornfield as he could. But the horse stood crunching, and his long lips quivered. The lollipop must taste so good, so sweet to him!

At that nice moment the two bobwhites came flying. They flew down to the two posts of the pasture gate to sit there and whistle "bobwhite, bobwhite." They had followed and found him! Ray told the horse about it. "Look, the bobwhites came, too. And it isn't all alone at all anymore, is it? You don't like to be all alone either, do you?"

The bobwhites flew away again, maybe because he'd just talked to the horse, and hadn't whistled back to them. Well, anyway, all you could do was whistle back to a bobwhite. You could talk to a horse! And you could feed him! Ray grabbed the first stalk of corn at the first fence post. The horse watched. But hard as Ray pulled the corn wouldn't come up.

Ray stooped way down and grabbed the cornstalk near its bottom. He strained and pulled. It was amazing how tightly the corn was grown in the ground. It wouldn't come at all. He tugged harder. Suddenly the corn let go and came up out of the ground with a big clump of roots, dirt and all. It happened so suddenly Ray tumbled over backward. The stalk of corn that was three times as tall as he fell over him. The tasseled tip fell against the barbed wire. The horse grabbed the tip of the cornstalk, pinched it between his lips, and pulled the whole cornstalk, roots, dirt and all, over Ray into his pasture. It was funny. Ray just lay there and laughed and looked up at the horse, but the horse immediately began to eat. Then Ray jumped up, because the horse was *that* hungry. He pulled up the next stalk of corn. It was hard and mighty and important work.

With the horse still eating the third and last stalk of corn at the first fence post, Ray ran to the next post. Here there were five stalks of corn! He tugged and strained, he grunted loudly so the horse would hear what important work he was doing for him. The horse did hear He came hurrying, without even finishing all of the last stalk of corn at the first fence post.

Oh, it was a game. Now it was a game. A good game! It was good for the horse, all that good food! Ray fell back with the cornstalk over him, even when he didn't have to—just to show the horse what hard work it was, and because it was such fun to have the horse drag the corn over him, lump of roots, lump of dirt and all. The horse did not eat the roots with the dirt on them—he just wanted clean corn!

Ray ran to the next fence post. He kept count. Now the horse had eaten seven, no, eight whole stalks of corn. He counted it out again on his fingers before he set to work at the third fence post.

Oh, it was a hurry and an excitment, because he was going to pull up the corn at every fence post all around the hilltop. "Oh, then you'll be full," he praised and promised the horse. "All full and round!"

But the work got harder; the big lumps of

113

dirt around the roots seemed to get heavier and heavier. Ray was getting tired from pulling up corn. And it looked as if the horse was getting tired from eating corn. He ate more and more slowly, and less and less of each stalk. At the fifth fence post he let the last cornstalk lie. He sniffed at it, he chewed the tip of one leaf just a little bit, but then he snorted, wheeled around, and walked to the gate. He stood at the gate, looked back, and seemed to be waiting for Ray.

Ray slowly walked to the gate. Oh, he was tired! It would be nice to sit on the gate—just sit and talk to the horse. He wondered if he dared. But Shirley dared, and she was a girl!

The gate wasn't nearly so wiggly and tipsy as Ray had expected. The horse stood tight against the gate. That held the gate steady, and climbing the boards was as easy as climbing a ladder. He threw one leg over and sat astride the gate. Now he was higher than the horse. It was a proud thing! Why, if he wanted, he could easily reach out and pat the horse's neck and his mane. Of course, he did not want to! He was awfully high, and awfully close to the big horse. It was so close. If he leaned down he could

114

almost whisper into the horse's ear. He said, "Hi, horse. I'm higher than you."

His saying "Hi, horse," suddenly made him think. He didn't even know the name of the horse!

He thought and thought about it while the horse stood quiet before him. The horse stood there swishing his tail back and forth against the gatepost. His head drooped, and his eyes were sleepy, and his lips had green corn stains. The old horse stood so sleepy Ray suddenly dared to reach out and touch his mane, just with his fingertips. "D'you know what?" he said. "I'm going to call you Rim—Thee-Rim. That's my other name, and I don't use it. Only Martin sometimes calls me Thee-Rim when he thinks he's funny." He chuckled. "Yeah—Thee-Rim—that's what I'm going to call you, because I don't know your name." He touched the horse's mane again, chuckled to himself, then said solemnly, "I baptize you—Thee-Rim." He laughed and laughed to hear himself say it. Oh, it was funny. He reached out once more to do it again. "I baptize you—Thee-Rim."

At that moment the horse snorted and tossed up his head. His neck knocked against Ray's outstretched hand. Ray grabbed wildly for the top board of the gate, but missed. He lost his balance. He fell forward—fell on the horse. He grabbed at the horse, his fingers wildly grabbing in the horse's mane. He clutched at it, then flung his arms around the horse's neck. He screamed out. In the stillness he could hear his scream go screaming out over the fields.

The horse did not move or toss his head. The old horse stood patiently still. He seemed to be waiting. With his arms clutching the neck of the horse, Ray tried to push himself back on the gate. He lay flat. His feet felt the top of the gate, but he couldn't seem to let go with his arms. He desperately pushed himself up into a sitting position, so he could reach for the gate the way Shirley had done. But his hands just grabbled more into the horse's mane. He clung to the mane, and there he sat—on the horse!

It was high and scary and cold and exciting and everything all together and at the same time. But now that the horse felt Ray sitting, he started forward, just as he'd done with Shirley. In his nicest, softest voice Ray hurriedly told the horse, "You don't have to give me a ride. You don't have to. I'll give you an apple."

116

The horse didn't listen. He *wanted* to give Ray a ride. And after a few more steps it wasn't so scary anymore, and then in a little while it became sort of scary fun. There they went! The horse walked along the fence, and he walked slow as slow. He even lifted his feet to step over the leftover stubs of cornstalks with their big lumps of roots and dirt. He didn't stumble, he was careful. Oh, he was careful!

It was wonderful, scary wonderful. Ray was proud, scary proud. In his nicest voice Ray praised the horse, but he kept a tight hold on the mane. The old horse did not seem to mind having the hair of his mane pulled. Oh, it was high! Now Ray dared to look up. He looked away from the horse. They were going around the hilltop. He could see over the corn. He could see a clump of trees below the hill far beyond the corn. And a road, and a big, red roof! Why, that must be the road that Grandpa lived on, the road the school was on. It was a big roof. It must be the roof of the school. Martin and Shirley were in the school, but he was riding a horse!

They came around the hill, and now over the stretches of corn he could see his own house.

118

He could see the roof and the top tip of the gable and the attic window. Mother was washing the attic window! He could see Mother! Ray almost yelled out, "Look, Mom. Mom, look!" Then he realized that while he could see her, Mother could not see him over the corn. And it was a secret! And he mustn't yell out and scare the horse. Oh, but it was a proud thing secretly to see Mother from the big horse that he was riding.

The horse kept going, and then they started around to the gate. The horse stopped along side the gate to let Ray off, the same way he let Shirley off. Then, like Shirley, Ray grabbed the top board of the gate and pulled himself off the horse. Once more astride the gate, he really praised the old horse. "Oh, you're careful. Oh, you're a good horse, Thee-Rim. It was fun. And I wasn't scared—only just at first."

He pulled the apple out of his pocket for Thee-Rim. Now that he'd ridden him, it wasn't scary to lay the apple in the cupped palm of his hand and hold it out to Thee-Rim. Thee-Rim's lips came quivering. They were soft! He felt the velvety softness as they lifted the apple out of his hand. He thrilled.

119

While Thee-Rim ate the apple, Ray pulled the lollipop out of his pocket and held it ready for him. Thee-Rim had to have the lollipop, too. Still, his own mouth was sort of dry from the ride around the pasture. He took a few quick licks, but then he gave it to Thee-Rim. He remembered to hang onto the stick.

Thee-Rim crunched and slobbered and spilled. And now Ray suddenly wanted to run home to Mother, even though he couldn't tell her about Thee-Rim, and couldn't tell her a thing about the big ride. Oh, it would be hard to do, never to tell! Still he had to run—run hard. He tried to explain it to Thee-Rim. "You know, from way up on your back I could see my mother. She was washing a window. So now I've got to run, because I've been gone so long. And if Mother knew I'd been riding you—well, she'd just die. Oh, not really," he hastily corrected. "That's girl talk. That's the way Shirley talks. Mother wouldn't really die and fall dead, but, oh, she'd be scared! She's awfully scared of all animals, even little ones! She'd never let me come here again."

He climbed down the gate. It still seemed hard to run away, even after explaining. But

Thee-Rim did not nicker or neigh. He just stood there, sleepy. That was because he'd eaten so much corn. Suddenly Ray just turned and ran, because he did not know how else to leave. He ran hard. Then midway down the lane the bobwhites came flying. But, oh, boy, he was running so fast the bobwhites had no time to land on a fence post to whistle. They just had to keep fluttering from fence post to fence post. But he had ridden a horse! Oh, boy! And now he could do it every day. Every day—this whole week! Well, not on Saturday and Sunday, because then Shirley and Martin were home. But every other day! Oh, boy!

"Oh, boy, oh, boy, oh, boy, oh, boy!" He yelled it, and danced down the lane.

CHAPTER 8 * THE HAT
IN THE LANE

"October-September," Mother was saying at the breakfast table. "September-October. Those months even sound as lovely as they are. Do you realize we've been living here for over a month, and every day has been sweet and sunny and serene? Why, we've hardly had any rain. Every day has been full of loveliness and longing, and a waiting smokiness lying over the fields. October-September is loveliness, but the rains will come, and then the winter."

It was Sunday. Everybody was in the kitchen, but Mother seemed to be talking to herself. At least nobody was listening. The words were lovely, Ray thought, even though Mother had said them backwards—for September came first. Then Dad began fussing about having to eat fried kippered herring for breakfast on Sunday just because Shirley and Martin insisted on it. "Oh, I'll eat it, I'll go along with it," Dad said to Mother. "This is Sunday for you, too. And if you have to fix something different for each one of us . . . What do you think your mother is?" he suddenly asked Shirley. "A short-order cook in a hamburg joint?"

Shirley got red spots on her cheek, and the red even ran down her neck. Martin looked down his nose. Ray knew they didn't know what to say, because all they wanted kippered herring for was the tin cans for boats.

"October-September," Mother said over at the stove. "It's nice to think of when you're frying kippered herring."

Dad interrupted to say to Ray, "I suppose, young man, you don't have to eat herring? Your mother will fix you something else."

"Oh, he doesn't mind kippered herring," Mother said. "He's been eating it three days running without making a fuss. But I'm poaching eggs for myself, so if Ray wants . . . "

Suddenly he wanted poached eggs with Mother, because she'd said that about October-September and haze and smokiness, and because it was so. The past week had been the loveliest of his life—riding Thee-Rim, feeding him corn, having an apple and a lollipop with Thee-Rim, and talking to him.

"Still, winter is coming," Mother said over and above the frazzling noises at the stove. "You just know it! Even the mice are leaving the fields. They're coming into our old basement by droves."

"It's the kippered-herring smell seeping out of every crack of this house that brings them in," Dad teased Shirley and Martin. "How many Santa Marias do you two need anyway?"

"What's all this about Santa Marias?" Mother asked as she put plates on the table.

"Oh, aren't you wise to it yet?" Dad said. "We have to eat kippered herring so they can have tin cans for boats to sail in the creek."

"*No!*" Mother exclaimed. "And me gagging every morning for that! Not another kippered herring comes in this house."

Shirley and Martin both gave Ray glum,

124

angry looks. They were mad at him all over again for having given away their secret to Dad. They were mad at Dad, too, for giving the secret away to Mother, so that now Mother knew they'd been fooling her. But they didn't dare look mad at Dad. They just gave Ray the mean looks.

Dad didn't notice. "What gets me," Dad said, "is that they don't bother to hunt up their tin-can boats when they sink. When our boats sank that Sunday morning, we hunted them up again after church, didn't we, Ray? We didn't make everybody eat kippered herring and sardines."

"On Sunday—you and Ray went sailing tin cans instead of going to church?" Mother spluttered.

"No, before and after church," Dad said. He acted like a naughty boy that had been caught. He looked at Ray, and tapped himself on the mouth. "Didn't Ray tell you? Well, I must say, he can keep a secret better than I can!"

Ray looked right at Martin and Shirley. Now they must know he could keep a secret and didn't tattle!

"This morning we'll all go to church together," Mother announced. "Oh, it's not to keep you from sailing boats, or anything like that," she hastily explained to Dad in a different voice. "It's that I'd like to start going to church again as a family, because I'd like Ray to go to Sunday School, too. And we're extra early this morning. And, well, I'd like to take a ride through the country together, because I feel in my bones there's going to be a change in the weather, and then winter will come, and all this fall beauty will be gone."

Dad was pleased, and agreed immediately. After breakfast was over, he made everybody hurry to get ready. Ray found it hard to hurry. He was puzzling hard. Now how was he going to get to Thee-Rim to feed him? He had expected to go to church with Dad, then after church, while Mother and Shirley and Martin were still at the second service, he'd planned to run up the lane and feed Thee-Rim. No, he'd even thought of telling Dad about Thee-Rim this Sunday—maybe even showing Thee-Rim to Dad, and asking Dad a hundred questions. Now with everybody going to church there'd be no chance afterward to feed Thee-

Rim. Thee-Rim would go hungry this whole Sunday. Just like that the whole plan was spoiled.

"Are you disappointed, Ray?" Mother suddenly said. "Don't you want to go to church with all of us? You're so poky and dreamy. Get those shoes on!"

"Yes, Mother!" he said. He stooped over his shoe, because he felt red, warm spots on his cheeks. Thee-Rim would go hungry all day. Thee-Rim wouldn't know it was Sunday, and everything was different on Sundays.

"You have to wear two shoes to church," Dad suddenly said right over him. "And you won't get the second one on by staring at the first one."

Dad didn't take the road to church they usually took. Dad said he wanted to go all around the cornfield, just to see how big it was and how far it went. Mother kept exclaiming and calling Dad's and Ray's attention to things she saw along the roads. Sitting in front between Dad and Mother, Ray couldn't see much except straight ahead. Shirley and Martin were whispering in the back seat, playing some sort

127

of silly game they were making up as they rode along. They didn't even bother to look at what Mom pointed out.

"Oh, look," Mother suddenly said, "they're beginning to cut the corn! Look at all the huge machinery. What a shame. There the corn lies all smashed down, and it stood so tall. But it had to come, didn't it? Fall and harvest time are here."

"Harvest time is really past," Dad said. "I noticed yesterday when I came home that they'd started cutting at the other end of the field, too. That way it won't be long, and it will all be down. High time, too. I was wondering when they were going to get started. Of course, now they just strip off the ears and mow the corn down. In my time we had to cut it by hand and set it in shocks, and it took weeks."

"Dad, you're just an old hick," Shirley said from the back seat.

"A hay-seed Hiram," Martin said. Then they both giggled. Dad was looking so hard at the corn and the big machinery he did not hear.

"Will they cut the corn all around our house, too, Dad?" Ray asked.

"All," Mother said. "Then we won't be liv-

128

ing in our green sea anymore. There'll just be
the raw fields and the flattened corn—and then
winter and snow."

"If they've started cutting from both ends
of the field," Dad said, "it looks to me they
should meet about where our house stands, and
that'll be the end."

"It's sort of sad," Mother said. "It stood so
tall and green and straight and sure. . . . But
we'd better start heading for church. It's getting that time." Everybody sat quiet for a while,
then Mother said to Ray, "This is the last time
you wear that hat. I don't know what pos-
sessed me to buy it just before fall, but it was
so cute."

Ray sat small and quiet between her and
Dad. Shirley and Martin were whispering and
giggling in the back seat, and that made Ray
think that now with them along, he would have
to sit between Dad and Mom in church. It
made it look as though he was so little he didn't
know how to behave in church. But Shirley insisted on it whenever she was with them. All
because when he was very small he'd once
talked out and laughed in church. Martin had
tickled him!

129

It had been awful. Shirley's face had gone red, even her neck. Mother had nudged Dad, and Dad, looking very grim and stern, had made him get up and move in between him and Mother. And all the people turning and looking!

Then thinking about that, suddenly the plan hit him! If he sat between Mother and Dad in church, without making any fuss about it beforehand, and if he asked Mom if he might go home with her and Dad right after church, without staying for Sunday School . . . Why, if she let him, then with Shirley and Martin in Sunday School, he could quickly grab an apple and run to Thee-Rim, and give Thee-Rim some corn. Oh, there'd be no time to pull up whole cornstalks. He'd just break some ears off the standing corn, and explain to Thee-Rim it was Sunday.

He sighed with delight. There was the whole plan, complete and thought out!

At that moment Dad said, "Why so quiet, Ray?"

"Dad," he said immediately, "in church may I sit between you and Mom?"

"Why? D'you want to keep me awake?" Dad asked. "What'd you do—bring a pin?"

Shirley and Martin laughed, but Mother slid her arm down from the back of the seat and put it around him. "I'd like that," she said. "I never get to go to church with you anymore."

Oh, he wished he could tell Mother about Thee-Rim. Just Mother! No, Dad, too!

He snuggled up against Mother. "May I go right home with you and Dad, and not go to Sunday School—just today?"

"Why?" Mother said softly. "Why don't you want to go to Sunday School, Raimie?"

Snuggled against her like that he did not mind her calling him Raimie in front of Martin and Shirley. Softly, so Martin and Shirley wouldn't hear, he told her, "I'd like to go down the lane, because they're cutting the corn, and it'll all be different."

It was true! Oh, it was also true that he wanted to bring Thee-Rim an apple and feed him corn, but that was next true, and he couldn't tell Mother about Thee-Rim.

Mother thought for a while. "Well, just for this time, Ray, yes. Just for a last walk in the lane among the tall corn. Tomorrow or the next day they'll have it all down, and then things won't be like this again until this time next year."

There it was. The whole plan complete—the plan that had almost planned itself. He sighed with relief, and settled down in the seat.

After church the plan didn't work out at all the way he had expected. He and Mother and Dad got back from church. Dad stopped the car at the back door. Mother got out, then she looked up in the sky, and said, "If you want a last walk up the lane in the corn, Ray, better hurry. It's going to rain."

Dad was studying the cornfield behind the house. Now he too looked up at the sky. "Yeah," he said, "it's sure going to rain. It'll be raining hard by the time I've got to get Martin and Shirley from Sunday School."

Dad and Mom kept standing in the yard looking at the sky and looking at the corn. They didn't move. Then Mother said, "I think I'd like a last walk among the corn myself. I've never been up that lane."

"Okay," Dad said. "Let's do that. But not until after I've had my coffee. We'll squeeze it in between the rain and the coffee."

"Better get going, Ray," Mother said. "And come right back. Don't run, and don't climb things in your Sunday clothes."

132

"No, Mother," he said dutifully. Dad and Mom stood there and watched. Once out of sight among the corn, Ray started running as hard as he could. Suddenly he stopped dead in his tracks. There was something at the skunk hole. Something stirred the dried cornstalks that poked up out of the hole. Something black and white. His heart in his throat, Ray tiptoed ahead a few steps, then stopped again. What if it was a skunk? Dad had said skunks were black and white—black and white stripes! Now he did not see it anymore. It must have scooted away into the corn.

What if the skunk had come home, and wanted to go down in its den, but couldn't because of the cornstalks? You couldn't explain that *you* hadn't stuck the hole full of cornstalks. Martin and Shirley had done it! You couldn't explain to a skunk that you'd always treated it with respect, and had only said nice things down into the hole—not mean things like Martin!

You couldn't explain anything to a skunk. Anyway, the skunk wasn't there anymore, but it was going to rain, and if he was still going to get to Thee-Rim . . . Desperately Ray half shut his eyes so that he would see only straight ahead. Then he charged past the skunk hole. He put his hand on top of his hat so it wouldn't fly off as he pounded hard up the lane.

Thee-Rim was waiting at the gate. He poked his head way over and held it down so Ray could stroke his soft nose and his long, bony face, and so he could nuzzle Ray's pocket for an apple. Thee-Rim just wouldn't believe Ray had no apple today. Ray pulled both pockets of his Sunday trousers inside out to show Thee-Rim. "It's Sunday," he explained, "and Sundays are different. I can't stay, and I've only got time to break off some ears of corn for you. I can't pull up corn today, because I can't get myself dirty."

Thee-Rim snorted and tossed his head up above the gate. Then just as suddenly his head shot out and he grabbed Ray's hat off his head. Ray jumped up and grabbed the hat with both hands, but Thee-Rim's big yellow teeth crunched down on the rim, and a piece tore out of the hat. It was a sickening feeling. Ray stood in open-mouthed dismay staring down at his hat. The ribbon hatband hung loose and wet. Thee-Rim chewed and munched his piece of the straw hat.

It was about the most dismaying thing that could have happened—and on Sunday! He couldn't even cry or scold or feel mean. It was hopeless, because there was nothing to be done about the hat. It would give everything away. It was so sad, Ray didn't go into the corn and break off ears for Thee-Rim. He just turned, and ran away. Thee-Rim didn't neigh or nicker after him. He was too busy eating the piece of hat.

Once Ray looked back, but he could not see Thee-Rim at the gate anymore. Then it began to rain. Just all of a sudden it began to rain. Without a warning or a sound the rain fell straight down out of the black sky. In one moment Ray was soaked. Now everything was hopeless and awful. He still held the ruined hat in his hand, and he still had to get by the skunk hole. Again Ray turned around. There behind him was the black and white thing, half hidden by a fence post. He could just see it in the streaming rain. It was behind him; it was following him. Now it was gone again.

What if it was the skunk, and the skunk was chasing him because it couldn't get in its hole in the awful rain? He could think of only one thing to do to show it wasn't his fault. Ray rushed up to the skunk hole, grabbed the whole armful of cornstalks, pulled them out of the hole and flung them to the ground. He looked back to see if the black and white thing were watching. But when he looked at the hole he saw that now the rain was washing straight down into it. And the skunk had seen him pull out the stalks!

He whirled around at a movement in the

136

corn. He grabbed up his hat, then suddenly he had a wonderful thought. The hat! He stooped and laid the bitten hat over the hole.

As Ray came running across the yard, the door opened and Mother started calling him. Behind her Dad bellowed out his name. Then they saw him. Mother held the door wide open and he stormed in, soaked and dripping with

mud all over. But the first thing Mother said was, "Where's your hat?"

There wasn't a thing he could think up to say. He felt his wet hair as if it were the first time he'd noticed his hat was missing. "Oh, it's in the lane," he said. "It rained so hard and I had to run, and . . ."

Dad and Mother looked at him. There was nothing to do but tell. Mother peeled the wet clothes off him. "Dad," he said, "you know that skunk hole I told you about? Well, the skunk came back. And it was a skunk, because he was white and black, and you said, 'Always treat a skunk with respect,' so I pulled all the cornstalks out of the hole for him, but then the rain rained in, so I put my hat over the hole for the skunk."

Mother said, *"What?"*

Dad laughed. "That's sure showing a skunk all the respect he can expect—leaving him your Sunday hat."

Mother was indignant. "Imagine leaving a perfectly good hat over a skunk hole!" she spluttered.

"You said yourself this was that hat's last Sunday," Dad reminded her.

"You would encourage him," Mother said. "But to fool around with a skunk!"

"Don't worry so," Dad said to Mother. "It couldn't have been a skunk. Not if it scooted away into the corn. Skunks don't scoot. Most likely it was just a young stray cat that got interested in rattling those dry cornstalks around. All the rest is Ray's imagination."

Mother kept shaking her head. "Boys!" she said. "Men! Your father would encourage you, and now I suppose you think you did something wonderful. Off to bed. It's for punishment, and to get you warmed through and through from that cold soaking. Giving your hat to a skunk! Even if it was a cat!"

Ray willingly went up the stairs, willingly put himself to bed, for the big secret about Thee-Rim was safe.

CHAPTER 9   *   RAIN

Ray came charging down the stairs, looking for Mother. She was sitting at the kitchen table having a cup of coffee all by herself. Ray pointed to the windows. "It's raining," he almost shouted at Mother. He must be way late. It must be Dad had already gone for the week, and Shirley and Martin were at school. Mother sat there with her lap full of clotheslines. "Good morning," she said.

"Mother, it's raining hard. I just woke up, and I looked out of my window, and the corn is all down. Everything is flat, and it's all wind and rain."

Even in the warm kitchen the sound of rain and wind against the windowpanes was ugly and cold. "Didn't you know?" Mother said. "No, that's right, you can sleep through anything. It must be that rain you got caught in yesterday scared them into getting busy. All that machinery we saw yesterday on the way to church—there it came from both ends of the field, and they worked all through the night. The machines were grinding and whining everywhere, and big trucks loaded with gleaming yellow ears of corn came and went. You could see everything. They had spotlights on everything. All that roaring and grinding and clanking, I didn't sleep a wink all night! Now there's still the wash to do."

"I never heard a thing," Ray said. "Why didn't you call me?"

"I thought of waking you. But then I was afraid you'd be so fascinated you wouldn't sleep all night. And sleep's more important. But now I'm sorry you didn't see it. It was quite a sight."

A new sweep of wind rattled the windows. Ray sat woefully looking at it. Now he couldn't go out to Thee-Rim. Mother'd never let him go out in rain like this. It wasn't the slightest use to ask. Helplessly he looked at the streaming, hazy-cold windows. Everything looked cold

141

and awful and nasty wet. Thee-Rim had had nothing to eat yesterday either, except a piece of straw hat.

"Well," Mother said, grabbling the three wound-up clotheslines out of her lap, and getting up slowly, "I was just going to the attic to string these lines to hang the wash. There's certainly no use waiting for this rain to stop. The radio said all day, maybe all week, rain mixed with sleet, then maybe even wet snow. It's a complete change in our heavenly fall weather. Just like that . . . Want to go up with me? You don't seem to be hungry yet. Anyway, it's so close to noon, and Dad said he might come home later on. He's at a sales conference this morning."

As they climbed up to the attic they heard the great roar of rain on the roof. The sound seemed to slam at them down the well of the attic stairway. Ray followed Mother across the thunderous attic. Mother went to the little window that overlooked the cornfield. There it lay in the day-dark rain—all the great field of corn. All the tall, straight corn, flat and limp with the rain lashing it and muddy water streaming over it. There it lay in the raw field in the cold, wet, nastiness.

The only thing that poked up anywhere were the fence posts. Ray strained to see the sharp hill where Thee-Rim must be. All he could see was the rain streaming dark over the fields.

"Isn't it sad and pitiful?" Mother said. "The corn stood so tall. It was like an army with banners, the tassel tips stirring and swaying. But there it lies beaten down into the mud and water." Mother sounded sad. She said it again. "It was like an army. Last night, too, when it was going down, it made me think of something from the Bible: 'The beauty is slain upon the high places. How are the mighty fallen.' "

Below in the raw, bare field a flock of pheasants came skulking single file, heads and wet tails held down to the pounding rain. The proud cock pheasant's long tail feathers dipped and dragged over the flat, wet corn, the corn that had fed them not hiding them now.

After the pheasants were gone from view the rain came lashing in hard, swift sweeps over the roof. The little window rattled with wind and clattered with rain. He and Mother stood looking up at the noise on the roof. Mother said it loud: " 'How are the mighty fallen.' "

"No, Mother," Ray begged. "No." He

144

wanted to cry.

Mother looked at him. "Oh, I'm sorry. Is it too awful, Raimie?" Mother sort of shook herself, then she said in a new, busy voice, "I think I'll wash today, anyway. A day like this it almost makes you glad to be in the old basement. There you see nothing."

In spite of themselves they both turned toward the little window, and there down in the field came the same little band of pheasants back again down the long row in the same way —skulking along with their beaten-down tails. "Ah, the poor animals whose home was in the corn," Mother said, "and now all the corn down . . . Come on, let's not stand here any longer. I've got the clotheslines, but I can see I'll need a hammer and some nails."

He turned with Mother from the window, and she must have thought he was following her, for she went straight down the attic stairway and didn't look around. He hadn't followed her. He couldn't. He stopped in the middle of the attic, helpless. He was standing here, but poor old Thee-Rim was standing in the wind and rain on the hill. There he stood in the cold windy wetness, and he'd had nothing

145

to eat all day yesterday, and he'd get nothing today. If it rained all week the way the radio had said . . .

It must be about the most awful thing to be hungry and have the rain raining down on you. That's what Dad had wished for the bull. "I hope you stay caught in the fence and it rains on you and your ugly head for two weeks!" Dad had yelled. But this was Thee-Rim! The good horse—Thee-Rim! And yesterday Thee-Rim had already been so hungry he'd bitten into the straw hat.

Mother's head appeared in the well of the attic stairway. He hadn't heard her come in the roaring, drumming of the rain. "Oh, did you decide to stay up here?" Mother said. "Dad called. He isn't coming home this noon after all. The sales conference is over but he couldn't get his car started. Dad's staying with it at the garage. If they can still get it fixed today he might go right on out of town."

He stared at Mother. Way back in his mind he had hoped that Dad would be home at noon so he could tell him, and Dad would do something about Thee-Rim.

Mother began to drive a nail up under the

slant of the attic roof. "Dad said he'd stay with the car until he was sure. But if it can't be fixed this afternoon he'll call, because then he wants to come home. He wants me to pick him up. . . . Well, once I get these nails driven, you can help me with the lines. And that's all I'll do. It's no sense starting the wash if I have to pick up your dad."

"Mother," he said, "may I go downstairs? I don't want to be up here anymore in all the rain." He bolted.

Downstairs Ray prowled from room to room. He couldn't be still. Mother had the big radio going in the living room and the little one in the kitchen, and in both rooms the same man on the radio talked about the weather. Ray opened the kitchen door to look out. The tug of the wind was so strong the doorknob was jerked out of his hand and the wind sent the door slamming against the outside wall. Ray had to lean far out to pull the door shut. Rain splashed down on his head and bent neck. The rain was nasty cold and crawly. It ran down his neck, it crawled coldly over his scalp in among his hair. In the kitchen he grabbed a dish towel and rubbed his head.

147

He raced up the stairs to the attic, and when he got there Mother was standing at the little window. "Mother," he said desperately, "when it rains, it rains on all the animals out there too, doesn't it?"

"Yes, of course, Raimie," Mother said. "Unless they have burrows or dens, or places to crawl under—or houses to get into like the mice in our basement."

"I don't mean wild animals," he said impatiently. "I mean big animals, like cows and horses."

"Why, naturally, Ray. You know that! When it rains it certainly has to rain on them, if they're out. But their owners don't usually let them stay out in weather like this. They bring them into their barns or stables."

"But if they don't," he said. "If nobody comes . . ."

"Well, horses and cows have thick hides and hair. They're somewhat protected."

Ray felt his damp hair. "Mother," he said impatiently, "even if horses have thick hides and hair, don't they still get cold in the rain? Won't they get sick? You put me to bed when I got wet in the rain yesterday so I wouldn't

148

get sick. I had clothes on. Isn't that almost the same as having a thick hide and hair? But I got all cold inside."

"Well, I suppose so," Mother said. "Yes, I must say they stand miserably in windy wet rain—all hunched and bowed, with their hindquarters turned to the cold wind. Still it's different, and they're not people. It must be different, because farmers do let horses and cows out of the stable in the dead of winter and in the snow. Sometimes all day and even nights. So it can't be it bothers them, the way it does people. Anyway most farmers keep them inside. . . ."

There was a sudden let up in the squally sounds of rain and wind. The quiet seemed almost complete for just a moment. In that moment the telephone shrilled downstairs.

"The phone!" Mother said. "That must be Dad."

Ray plunged down the stairs, not waiting for Mother. But the telephone in the living room hung dead and still. Then the same phone sounds shrilled out again. It was a telephone on the radio. It wasn't their phone at all!

Mother came into the room. "No!" she said. "All that running for a stage telephone. With

149

no sleep at all, I'm certainly in no mood to keep running up and down a couple of stairways. Maybe you'd better stay down here, in case your dad calls. I'll go and get the attic ready for the clotheslines."

Ray hurried to the living room window. It was as if he couldn't stay away. He thought Mother had gone, but when he turned to go to the other window she was in the doorway watching him. "What makes you so restless?" she said. "Is it because you can't go out to play?"

Ray nodded.

"Why don't you turn on the TV and watch that?" Mother suggested.

"Mother," he suddenly said, "may I go play in the garage?"

"In the garage?" Mother said. "What would you do there?"

"I . . . I'd . . . Oh, I could build a big fort or something with Dad's boxes and stuff," he thought up desperately.

"I should say not," Mother said. "You know you're not supposed to touch Dad's boxes. Why don't you watch TV, if you can't think of anything better than that to do with yourself?"

Mother stood there waiting. He turned on the television and settled himself into a deep chair. Then Mother went.

The television warmed up, and the sound and the picture came on in the midst of something. It must be funny. Everybody was laughing, and everything was bright and sunny. It was horrible! He didn't like the people. He felt mean toward them laughing in the sunshine. He didn't want them to laugh. He jumped up and turned the television off. Then the sound of the rain driving against the windows was in the living room again. The telephone stayed dead and quiet. Ray ran from the room, wanting to run up to Mother to tell her about Thee-Rim. He couldn't. He couldn't tell Mother. She couldn't do anything in this weather. And then if she found out he'd ridden Thee-Rim all last week! Shirley had said Mother would just die if she found out she and Martin were riding a horse. But if she found out *he'd* ridden a horse . . .

A horrible thought struck him. If Dad didn't come home, if the car got fixed and Dad went on out of town without first coming home, then he couldn't tell anybody. He couldn't do anything. If it rained all week, and the rain turned to snow . . . In his desperation the thought struck him. He could do what he'd said to Mother—go to the garage, not to build a fort with the boxes, but to move all the boxes out of the stable. If he couldn't lift them, he'd drag them. Then there'd be a stable for Thee-Rim. Thee-Rim would be under a roof, walls around him, even a window. The rain would rain down on the roof and outside the window, but Thee-Rim would be all warm and dry in the stable.

It was a marvelous thing to think. Why, if Dad did come home, he'd have the stable all ready, he'd tell Dad, and Dad would go out and get Thee-Rim and put him in the stable. He wanted it so badly for Thee-Rim, it seemed it just had to be done, right now, right away.

The next moment everything sagged within him. It was no use to ask Mother. She wouldn't let him. He looked at the television. He ran to it and turned it on loud. If he could do it now —run to the garage while Mother was busy in the attic. It seemed to him if he got it all done, got the stable all ready for Thee-Rim, then it just had to be that Thee-Rim would come to the stable.

152

His raincoat was hanging near the top of the basement stairway, his boots were standing on the bottom step. He pulled on his boots, and nervously buttoned the raincoat. He sneaked up the basement steps and stole through the kitchen very softly with very long strides. Mother was still hammering. He eased the kitchen door open, but the fierce wind caught it again. It flew out of his hand. He lunged after it to catch it before it slammed against the wall. The jerk of the door was so swift it carried him with it, pulling him off his feet. He lost his hold on the doorknob, tumbled headlong, and slid face down into a big puddle of muddy water. He lay there, stunned by the surprising swiftness of the happenings. He felt the cold water from the puddle running up his pants' legs. He raised his head and bawled. In his alarm and fright and shock, he pushed himself up. Dripping water and mud he stumbled back into the kitchen. Mother stood there. Her face was terrible. She pulled the kitchen door shut, then she stepped back. "And what did you think you were going to do?" she asked.

"Play in the garage," he said in a little voice. "Build a fort." He started to cry. He started toward Mother.

153

"No, stay right there on the doormat," Mother said. "Take off that raincoat and those boots. Get yourself undressed."

He fumbled with the raincoat. Mother didn't come to help. Her face was stern and red and displeased. "This I don't like one little bit, Ray. Not one little bit. You deliberately planned this. You turned the TV way up, so that I would think you were watching. You went down to the basement to hunt up your boots and raincoat to deliberately disobey me and go out in the garage anyway and play with the boxes. Now, young man, get all undressed and get yourself upstairs and into bed, and you'll stay there until I say you may come out. And this time it's for nothing but punishment. Maybe when I'm ready to come up to your room, you may be ready to tell me what's bothering you, and what you are keeping so secret from me."

"I'm ready now," he sobbed. Now it was so hopeless he wanted to tell Mother everything.

Mother shook her head. "Put on your pajamas when you get upstairs."

She didn't come near. He had to turn away and go naked and shivering and miserable up the stairs—all alone.

CHAPTER 10 * THE MAN
ON THE HILL

Ray awoke with a start. Mother was standing in the bedroom doorway talking to him. He'd been asleep! He blinked his eyes and tried to get his woolly mind to think.

It was amazing. He'd gone to sleep! He'd had to go to bed at noon, and maybe because in bed in your pajamas you were so helpless you couldn't even try to do anything—he'd just gone to sleep. He remembered lying staring up at the ceiling and thinking helpless things about Thee-Rim, and listening to the drum-drone of the rain against the windowpanes, and then he must have fallen asleep—at noon!

155

"Well?" Mother said. "Wide awake now? It can't be your conscience bothered you too much if you could sleep like that after the way you behaved. Do you know how long you have slept? I've been up here three times. You slept through the noon hour and slept away a good share of the afternoon. I had to wake you now because Dad called. The car can't be fixed to-day after all. There was more wrong than they figured. So now he called and wants me to come pick him up."

Ray sat up eagerly, waking and fully brightening at the news. Dad was coming home after all. Now he could tell Dad about Thee-Rim. Dad would know what to do.

"So," Mother went on saying, "after I've picked up your Dad in town, I'll drive around and pick up Martin and Shirley. School should be just about out then."

Ray threw the covers back, but Mother shook her head. "No, you're not coming along right out of a warm bed after that cold soaking you had in mud water. If you're hungry I'll bring you something to eat. But here you stay. And don't you dare to go out to that garage! I'm taking your boots and raincoat with me.

156

I'm sorry, Ray, but it's just that I can't trust
you."

He lay back and stared at Mother in dismay.
Dad would be home, but he was coming home
with Martin and Shirley. Then how could he
tell Dad about Thee-Rim? But if he didn't tell,
the night would come, and there'd be Thee-
Rim in the rain and the wind on the black
hill. . . .

"Well," Mother said, "do you want me to
bring you something to eat?"

He nodded. Luckily Mother turned around
and went down without asking him what he
would like. He wouldn't have been able to
think of a thing. All he could think of was
Thee-Rim, and the night coming, and everybody home so he couldn't do anything.

Mother brought him a sandwich and milk. She set the plate down beside the bed. "I have to hurry if I'm still going to be in time to pick up Martin and Shirley after picking up Dad." Now I want you to stay in bed. When I come home I'm coming up, and you and I will have a long talk."

He waited only long enough to hear the sounds of the car backing out of the garage, then he jumped out of bed. He stole down to the kitchen in his pajamas. Mother had washed out his muddy clothes. She'd set a chair before the register, and had hung the clothes over the back of the chair to dry. They were still damp. He pulled them on. He'd get wet again anyway. And he'd get punished—oh, he'd get punished more than he'd ever been punished before—if he went out. But he had to go out. He had to!

He had just hastily thought up something to tell Mother when he'd told her he wanted to play with Dad's boxes in the garage, but now it was a firm plan. He was going to lift and drag all Dad's boxes out of the stable and get it ready for Thee-Rim. Then he was going to get Thee-Rim. Somehow he'd open the pasture gate and let Thee-Rim out. Somehow, some

158

way. But it all had to be done before Dad, Mother, and Shirley and Martin came home. It all had to be finished. Then there Thee-Rim would be in their stable. Oh, it would all come out, the whole story, the whole secret, but Thee-Rim would be in the garage and out of the wind and the rain. Somehow he couldn't believe that anybody would take Thee-Rim out of the garage and take him back to his cold, wet, windy pasture.

Ray shivered as the damp clothes clung to his warm body. He didn't look for his shoes. In his bare feet he went to the basement to hunt for anything he could wear in the rain. In the basement, folded away in a box, he found an old pink raincoat of Shirley's. Under it was a pair of pink boots Shirley had worn as a little girl. He wrestled his bare feet into the boots. The raincoat had a hood. He pulled it over his head, then hurried out of the house. Nobody would see him in a girl's pink raincoat and boots—nobody except Thee-Rim.

This time he did not try to hang onto the door lest it pull him off his feet and fling him down in the puddle again. He let the door fly, and went out into the hard rain. He forced the door shut with his shoulder. The rain lashed down on him. It hurt through the raincoat and through his shirt. It was such a thin raincoat.

In the garage he pulled off the raincoat and set to work. Once he was pulling and tugging and straining at the boxes the thing he was doing seemed less scary. The dull dread in the pit of his stomach filtered away in the hard work. The sweeping sounds of rain were thunderous in the hollow garage, but he hardly paid any attention to it in the struggle with the piled boxes. He was amazed how fast the stable was emptying. The boxes on one side had been piled higher than the window, but already the window was cleared. Thee-Rim's window! He moved the boxes only far enough back from the stable so that Thee-Rim would be able to walk by. Then it was done. There was the stable, empty and bare, and there the cleared wooden floor for Thee-Rim to stand on. Now he listened to the rain on the roof. It wasn't raining hard now. He pulled on the raincoat, and pulled the pink hood far over his head to shelter his face. He slid the garage door wide open, leaving it that way for Thee-Rim to walk through.

160

In the hollow, worn lane the runneling water in the tractor ruts was racing almost as fast as the water did in the creek. The straw hat lay squashed near the skunk hole. A truck must have gone over it. Ray struggled on past the skunk hole. He bent low, but the rain found his face, lashed his face. The rain hurt as if it had little pieces of ice in it. The water came up cold and squashy through a leak in one of Shirley's old boots, and his foot was heavy and numb with water. The rain hurt his back and his arms and his shoulders right through the raincoat. There seemed to be bigger pieces of ice in the rain, sharp and cutting. But there was the gate, and he stumbled on.

Sheltered a little by the gate, he lifted his hooded head and peered between the gate boards up the rain-swept hill. Thee-Rim wasn't on the hill. There was nothing there but wind and rain. Oh, but Thee-Rim would be behind the hill to be sheltered a little from the wind.

"Thee-Rim!" he yelled. "Thee-Rim!"

He didn't wait. He clambered up the boards of the gate, and undid the loop of chain that held the gate to the fence post. He clambered down as fast as he could. He tugged and

161

strained to get the gate up out of the wet mud that had washed down the hill. The bottom board was sunk in the mud. He strained and grunted, half crying. But with all his efforts the bottom board did not even stir in the mud. Muddy water gurgled over his boots. He tried putting his shoulder under one of the boards. Nothing moved, and his shoulder hurt and flamed with pain. Helplessly he peered through the gate up the hill, helplessly yelling out, *"Thee-Rim!"*

As if he had heard, there over the top of the hill Thee-Rim came. But there was a man with Thee-Rim! A man in a black, long, furry bear-skin coat was walking beside Thee-Rim. They came down the hill walking tight together. Ray held his breath, but through the rain he saw, and through the rain he yelled it out—"Grand-pa!" It was Grandpa in a furry black coat. Then the great surprising realization that took Ray's breath away—it was Grandpa's horse. Thee-Rim was Grandpa's horse! Grandpa had come to take Thee-Rim from the pasture in the awful weather. He bawled it out through the gate, "Grandpa, Grandpa, Grandpa!"

The old man coming down the hill with the

horse peered through the rain, wonderment in his face. "Oh," he called out, "it's my little boy. It's little Ray. What are you doing here in this terrible weather?"

Ray laughed excitedly. He had to laugh, because just as Grandpa said "terrible weather," the squally rain stopped.

"Grandpa," Ray said in his amazement, "I didn't know he was your horse. I didn't know, Grandpa." He whirled around and looked down the hill. And now, with the corn down, the tall corn not hiding anything anymore, he saw below the sharp hill, the hollow with the clump of trees, and Grandpa's little white house. He could even see the fallen shed. "I didn't know Thee-Rim belonged to anyone. I didn't know he belonged to you, Grandpa, so I fed him corn every day." In his relief and wonderment the words tumbled over each other.

"You did that?" Grandpa said. "You were the one? I wondered at all the stubs of cornstalks with roots lying all around the pasture."

"I didn't know you fed him, too, Grandpa," he apologized.

"No, I didn't feed him. I couldn't—I've been

163

sick. I shouldn't be here, but the poor old horse
shouldn't either. No, I was going down the
road to the neighbors that have a telephone, to
have a truck come and pick up the old horse
and take him away." Grandpa suddenly leaned
hard against the gate. "I shouldn't have come
up here first. I suppose I just had to see the old
horse once more. But that hill, and this wind."
He shook his head wearily, and leaned against
the gate. "If Grandma finds out I sneaked out
of bed in this weather . . ." He shook his head
again. His face was white.

Ray looked up at the old man in wonder.
Grandpa had come out of bed to go to Thee-
Rim, and he'd got out of bed to go to Thee-
Rim. It was wonderful! He did not want to
think about that other thing—Grandpa's call-
ing on the phone for them to come to take
Thee-Rim away in a truck, even though
Grandpa thought he had to do it because the
shed was down and he had no place for Thee-
Rim.

"Grandpa," he said urgently, "will you help
me open the gate?"

Grandpa was coughing. He put his arm
against the gate and his forehead against his

164

arm, and coughed terribly. "It's my asthma," Grandpa gasped at last. "And climbing the hill. I wish I were home." He sounded like a tired little boy.

"Grandpa," Ray urged, "help me open the gate, because I'm going to take Thee-Rim home. We've got a stable. But I couldn't open the gate."

Grandpa lifted his head and stared at Ray. "You came to get the old horse to put him in your stable?"

"Yes, Grandpa," Ray said. "We've got a stable in our garage, and I made it all ready for Thee-Rim."

"Do your father and mother know?" Grandpa asked.

Ray had to say, "No."

Grandpa started to shake his head, then he looked hard at Ray. "Little Ray," he said, "why don't we? Why don't we do exactly that—put the old horse in your stable? Only a little fellow like you would ever have thought of it! But even if it's just for tonight—why not? I can't make it from here to the neighbor's phone. I know that now. I'll have all I can do to make it back home. Yes, we'll do it for tonight. You tell

165

your dad when he comes home to come and see me. If he doesn't want the horse there, then he can call the truck to come in the morning. . . .

Grandpa got a coughing spell again. He leaned hard against the gate. Finally, Grandpa wiped his eyes and his mouth, and sort of whispered, "I'll open the gate for you, and then I'll go home down the hill. Promise you'll tell your dad to come and see me as soon as he gets home."

Even Grandpa had to struggle to lift the gate high enough so it would slide open over the mud. But Thee-Rim didn't wait. The moment the gate opened a little he stuck his head through, then he pushed his chest through, and just shoved the gate open wide. Grandpa said, "Whoa," and Thee-Rim stopped. "Can you ride?" Grandpa asked.

"I can get on him from the gate," Ray said. Grandpa backed Thee-Rim alongside the gate. Ray climbed to the top, dropped on to Thee-Rim, and caught hold of his mane.

"Tell your dad I'm sick, and that I had all I could do to make it back home. That's why I did this crazy thing of letting you take my old horse home. Tell him . . ." Then Grandpa was seized by a fit of coughing, but suddenly

166

he just lifted his hand and brought it down on Thee-Rim. At the slap, Thee-Rim started ahead.

" 'Bye, Grandpa," Ray said. " 'Bye. I'll tell Dad right away."

Grandpa held up his hand, and Thee-Rim walked on down the lane. He walked carefully, picking his footing in the rutted, streaming, muddy lane, and he didn't look back at Grandpa. Then the rain lashed down again, and Ray had to lean out over Thee-Rim's neck, and cling to his mane, and almost lie flat, and he couldn't look back at Grandpa either. It began raining still harder. The sky was so black that the water in the lane around Thee-Rim's big white feet looked black. The rain washed over Ray and over Thee-Rim.

In the squally darkness that swept over them, something dark came up the far end of the lane toward Ray and Thee-Rim. At that moment, maybe because the ice in the rain was hurting him, Thee-Rim tried to run a little, but he stumbled and slipped in the mud under the water. He threw up his head, coughed and snorted, and walked again. Ray peered from

167

under his hood over Thee-Rim's head. Down
the lane lights turned on. It was a car—their
car! Now the headlights went out. They'd seen
him and Thee-Rim. And now as the dark car
came on he could see two white faces peering
through the windshield right behind the swishing windshield-wiper blades. Then the car
stopped, the door opened—Mother got out!
The car backed away down the lane; Mother
came running toward him and Thee-Rim. But

she slipped in the mud that had been chewed up by the tractors and trucks. To his horror she fell headlong in the mud and the water. She jumped right up again. She just let the mud and water drip. It even dripped from her fingertips, but Mother came running on. As she neared Thee-Rim Mother began to walk very slowly; she began to talk to Thee-Rim in the nicest, sweetest voice. "Good old horse," she said. "Sweet old careful horse. Take it easy now. Don't be alarmed about me. Everything's fine —Raimie's fine, you are fine—everything's fine."

Thee-Rim kept coming on. He wasn't excited a bit. Then as he walked past Mother she jumped and reached and grabbed his mane. "Steady now," Mother said softly up to Thee-Rim's ear. "You've got to be the one to have the sense here. Easy now . . . Ray," she said in another voice, "don't be afraid, and if you think you might fall, quickly grab my shoulder."

Ray couldn't answer her. He sat mute with fear that now Mother would turn Thee-Rim around and take him back to his pasture. Mother didn't. She just walked on with Thee-

169

Rim. Mother wasn't afraid of Thee-Rim; she wasn't afraid of a great big horse! She was afraid of mice—but not of a horse. She just was afraid for him, because she did not know he could ride Thee-Rim. She didn't know he'd ridden Thee-Rim for a week.

"Mother," he started to tell her, but at that moment the car finished backing out of the lane, turned in the road, and went up their driveway. Suddenly there was the hollow, awful fear that was what Mother was going to do —turn around in the road and take Thee-Rim back up the lane to the pasture.

"Mother," he cried out, "Thee-Rim is Grandpa's horse. I didn't know. Grandpa was there in this awful weather to get Thee-Rim out of the pasture, but Grandpa didn't have any place to take Thee-Rim because the shed is still down. Mother, I had to get the stable ready, because I knew Thee-Rim. I fed him every day. I knew about Thee-Rim in that pasture in the awful weather with nothing to eat. I told Grandpa we had a stable, and Grandpa said for Dad to come and see him. And Mother, the stable is all ready, and now it can rain but the rain can't rain on Thee-Rim. And Mother, Grandpa is sick . . ."

"Oh, Raimie," Mother said. "Why didn't you tell me. Why did you have to keep it a secret? Don't you think if you'd told me I'd know you'd have to go out and do something for the horse. Don't you think I'd have gone with you?"

He simply said, "No, I didn't know, Mother." For now they were at the road. But Mother didn't turn Thee-Rim around to go back up the lane. She didn't—she didn't. She led him across the lawn toward the garage, and Dad stood in the wide open doorway of the garage with Martin and Shirley. There they stood in a row. Mother led Thee-Rim right up to the doorway, then she suddenly reached up, grabbed Ray under the arms, and just let Thee-Rim walk from under him. Thee-Rim walked on through the wide open door into the garage. He was so big he almost scraped the top of the doorway. It was amazing how big he became in the garage, now that he wasn't in the big fields anymore. Now it seemed enormous, the thing he—Ray—had done in taking Thee-Rim from the field into the garage. Dad, Martin and Shirley stood aside for Thee-Rim, and Thee-Rim walked past them. Thee-Rim just snorted once, tossed his big head, and walked right into

171

the empty stable—as if he belonged, as if he'd known all about it all the time! When he was in the stable he turned his head alongside his body and looked at all of them. And nobody said a word. But Mother stood behind Ray and laid her hands on his shoulders. Still nobody said anything, but then Dad said at last to Ray, "D'you know what he's saying? He's saying, 'Well, come on. Don't just stand there. Bring me something to eat. Bring me some straw for this stable. I'd like to lie down sometime after standing all night and all day in that miserable rain! What's the matter with you? Get a move on!' "

Ray began shivering. He shivered all over, his shoulders shook under Mother's hands. He began laughing, but he laughed high and shrill like a very little boy. Dad wasn't angry. Dad wasn't going to take Thee-Rim back to the awful pasture. Nobody was going to take Thee-Rim back. And Dad had talked about food and about straw. Dad wasn't angry. Nobody was angry, just when he should have been punished the most of all! But if he didn't stop laughing he would start crying—he knew. And Shirley and Martin were looking so queerly from Thee-

Rim to him. Martin's mouth was a little bit open.

He ran. He ran right from under Mother's hands on his shoulders. He tore to the house. He couldn't cry in front of Shirley and Martin. But he turned and raced back. "Dad," he yelled out, "Grandpa is sick. Grandpa said for you to come and see him right away about Thee-Rim."

"Leave it to me, sailor. Just leave it me. But you get in the house and get those clothes off and take a hot bath. You, yes, and Mother, too. You're both a mess. But now you've got to get warm and dry, and Mother tells me you haven't eaten a thing all day. While you do that, I'll jump in the car and go to see Grandpa. And, Ray, if Grandpa will let us, isn't it much better to keep the horse here than to put up that shed? Who can put up a shed in this kind of weather?"

Ray broke away. He tore to the house. He had to cry, but not in front of Martin and Shirley. Mother came on behind him.

In the house he didn't have time to begin to cry, because he'd begun to talk. Talk and talk, and tell Mother everything, everything! He

talked all the time Mother undressed him, even
while they walked up the stairs, and when
Mother put him in the bathtub. He told
Mother everything. How from the first her
school game had been no good. Then he'd
found Thee-Rim. And Thee-Rim was such a
smart horse he could understand everything, so
he had told Thee-Rim everything, because he
hadn't known he could tell Mother about
Thee-Rim—not when Mother was afraid of
mice and bugs and things in the grass.

Mother just listened and didn't say anything. She was rubbing him with a big, dry towel so that his skin on the outside began glowing the way everything was glowing inside of him. Mother rubbed so hard he couldn't stand still, but just the same he proudly told Mother how amazed he had been that she hadn't been even a little bit afraid of Thee-Rim, a big horse.

Then Mother smiled. "Didn't you know?" she said. "No, you didn't know. But I had a horse when I was a little girl! Oh, it was just an overgrown pony, but I rode him, and loved him, and took care of him. And when you love something you aren't afraid of it. You have to do everything for it. I understand, Raimie, you had to do everything for your Thee-Rim. But you and I will have a talk later. Right now it's my turn in that bathtub. You look so glowing and bright, I'm envying you. So you go now. It's my turn for a hot bath."

Naked and laughing he ran from the room, but he turned, and through the closed door he begged, "I don't have to go to bed, do I, Mom? I mean, can't I wait for Dad to come back from Grandpa? Then I'll go to bed, Mother, and I'll stay and stay there."

Inside the bathroom, over the noise of the

draining water, he heard Mother laugh. "You're a schemer," she said through the door. "All right, put on your pajamas and bathrobe and slippers. Now get along with you before you get cold again—naked beggar outside my door!"

He laughed and ran. But after he'd dutifully put on his pajamas and bathrobe and slippers, he couldn't be still. He ran to the bedroom window. The rain had stopped, but the garage door was closed, and although Thee-Rim was inside he heard and saw nothing. It must be that Shirley and Martin had gone with Dad to Grandpa and Grandma.

He couldn't be still. He had to see more. He tore up to the attic. He hopscotched and danced along the whole attic, danced all the way to the attic window. He had to see more, he had to see everything.

The rain had stopped and the day had brightened. Then as he stood at the attic window, there came the sun. There came the rim of the sun peering from under a faraway black bank of clouds in the west. The rays of the evening sun brightened the fields, but the fields lay drifting with cold fog and haze.

There—it was as if through the haze—by the

sun's evening brightness he could see Thee-Rim's far away little hill. It seemed to him in the haze and the fog drifting over the hill as if the hill were almost dancing. He had a wonderful thought, a most wonderful thought there high in the attic. He thought that now it looked as if the hill were dancing. It must be the little hill rejoiced and danced and also sang because poor old Thee-Rim was no longer on the bare hill.

In the excitement of his imaginings he had to go hopscotching through the attic again. He had to dance, too—all through the attic and back to the window. He danced and he sang. And then he sang words—the words that came singing up out of him.

"October," he sang. "September," he sang. "October-September, September-October. And Nina and Pinta and Santa Maria. October-September, and Grandpa and Grandma. And the little white house over Thee-Rim's hill. And the rain can rain, but the rain can't rain on Thee-Rim anymore. No more, no more. No more, forever more."

He hadn't heard Mother come up the stairs. He thought she was still in the bath. But there Mother was. "What were you singing, Raimie? Sing it again. Sing it once more."

But it wasn't a song that you knew. It was a song that had just sung itself for you. He stood and tilted his head and listened as if to the words, but the words of his song wouldn't come anymore.

Mother stood waiting, so then he just said to her, "I'm here. Grandpa and Grandma are there. And Thee-Rim is in our stable. And the rain can rain but the rain can't rain on Thee-Rim anymore, ever more. . . ."

There was the sound of the car in the yard. With Mother he ran to the attic window. Martin had shoved the garage door wide open, and Dad drove the car into the garage. But the trunk of the car was loaded with a bale of hay and a bale of straw! Dad and Martin began dragging a big white bag out of the back seat of the car. A whole bag of oats, a bag full of oats for Thee-Rim!

Shirley looked up and saw Ray and Mother at the high attic window. "Ray, Raimie," she yelled, "it's your horse. Grandpa said it was your horse. Grandpa says if we want to keep him, he's your horse!"

"Boy, are you a lucky pup!" Martin yelled, and Martin sounded jealous. "We can keep him in our stable in winter, and in Grandpa's pasture in summer. Boy, were you lucky!"

"D'you see what we've got for your horse, sailor?" Dad tilted his head way back and stood there grinning. "Enough hay and straw for him to get lost in—and a big bag of oats. We'll build a crib and we'll stuff it full of hay, but first he's going to have a whole measure of oats. And d'you know what? All you have to do, Grandma and Grandpa said, now that you know the way, is come and visit them whenever the weather is nice, and tell them all about Thee-Rim."

"What ever made you think of calling him Thee-Rim?" Martin yelled. "Golly, how'd you come to think of it?"

But Mother gently led Ray away from the window. "Maybe you want to go to your room, and sit and cry just a little?" she said very softly.

He stopped before her at the top of the attic stair. He looked up at Mother. He said, as if just now he knew it for the first time, "Thee-

179

Rim is my horse, and he's in our garage, and the rain can't rain on him anymore. . . . But Mom," he urged, "I've got to go see him. I've got to see everything they're doing for him."

Mother nodded. "We'll get all bundled up and watch them doing things for Thee-Rim. And then, who knows—maybe once we get Thee-Rim fattened up a bit, and we get a saddle and bridle, and you promise me you won't keep secrets from me anymore—who knows, maybe I'll even teach you to ride Thee-Rim properly."

He stood rooted, he stood mute, but then he flew at Mother and hugged and kissed her.

Mother softly said, "I just now thought of it. Let's you and I do something for Thee-Rim, too. There are scrub brushes and a pailful of rags in the wash corner in the basement. While they're fussing with cribs and straw and hay, let's you and I rub Thee-Rim down and make him all dry and white and warm—the way I rubbed you all warm with the towel."

Speechlessly he stared at Mother, then he turned and tore down the stairs to get the scrub brushes and the pail of rags.

180

Format by Nancy Etheredge
Set in Linotype Baskerville
Composed by American Book–Stratford Press
Printed by Murray Printing Co.
Bound by The Haddon Craftsmen, Inc.
HARPER & ROW, PUBLISHERS, INCORPORATED